The Duke's Magnificent Obsession

The Hellion Club, Book Six

by Chasity Bowlin

ARE YOU SIGNED UP FOR DRAGONBLADE'S BLOG?

You'll get the latest news and information on exclusive giveaways, exclusive excerpts, coming releases, sales, free books, cover reveals and more.

Check out our complete list of authors, too!

No spam, no junk. That's a promise!

Sign Up Here

www.dragonbladepublishing.com

Dearest Reader;

Thank you for your support of a small press. At Dragonblade Publishing, we strive to bring you the highest quality Historical Romance from some of the best authors in the business. Without your support, there is no 'us', so we sincerely hope you adore these stories and find some new favorite authors along the way.

Happy Reading!

CEO, Dragonblade Publishing

Additional Dragonblade books by
Author Chasity Bowlin

The Hellion Club Series
A Rogue to Remember (Book 1)
Barefoot in Hyde Park (Book 2)
What Happens in Piccadilly (Book 3)
Sleepless in Southampton (Book 4)
When an Earl Loves a Governess (Book 5)
The Duke's Magnificent Obsession (Book 6)
The Governess Diaries (Book 7)
Making Spirits Bright (Novella)
All I Want for Christmas (Novella)

The Lost Lords Series
The Lost Lord of Castle Black (Book 1)
The Vanishing of Lord Vale (Book 2)
The Missing Marquess of Althorn (Book 3)
The Resurrection of Lady Ramsleigh (Book 4)
The Mystery of Miss Mason (Book 5)
The Awakening of Lord Ambrose (Book 6)
Hyacinth (Book 7)
A Midnight Clear (A Novella)

The Lyon's Den Connected World
Fall of the Lyon
Tamed by the Lyon
Lady Luck and the Lyon

Pirates of Britannia Series
The Pirate's Bluestocking

Prologue

May, 1816

A HEAVY BLANKET of snow, nearly ten inches deep and crusted with ice, lay over the land. More snow would come yet. But storm or no, there were people on the estate that required feeding. And that meant hunting for fowl or game as much as possible given the dismal return on crops for the previous year. The last thing they needed was an uprising or riot brought about by hunger. They were not so far removed from the Terror—the French Revolution and all the destruction it had wrought. With food scarce, taxes soaring, and struggles all around, there had been too many such events of late. As duke, it was his duty to see to the welfare and the support of his people when they were unable to do so themselves, whatever the reasons might be. And the three young men who accompanied him that day needed to learn that valuable lesson, as well. It would all fall to them one day.

Watching them, it was apparent that they were far more interested in playing in the unexpected snow than anything else. But they were young. Two of them stood nearly a head taller than the third, nearly identical in face and form. Light brown hair and easy smiles with a loose-limbed grace that hinted at natural athleticism. They were like their mother. Meanwhile, the smaller boy, with his coal black hair and slighter frame was much like him. He was still truly a child, even as his brothers were moving into that strange space between boy and man.

Six years separated them, the future Duke of Hargrieve, his twin and their younger brother—his sons. Twins by the name of Brendan and Bancroft had satisfied the requisite heir and spare that were deemed acceptable for a man of his station. Two other children had followed—both sons—and both had perished in the birthing process. It was a fact for which he and his wife had both grieved, though clearly she had taken it to heart much more.

But it was Barrett, his last child, who had thrived from birth, though the cost had been great. The duchess had succumbed to a fever days following their youngest son's birth. Because of that, it was Barrett who worried him the most.

In the years since, it had just been the four of them, struggling in a household devoid of any feminine touch. Barrett had never known his mother's love, never known what it was to be adored in the way that she certainly would have done had she lived. But Brendan and Bancroft, they recalled that love. They'd had it for years and it had given them a kind of self-assurance that he feared his younger son might never have.

Of course, the lack of female influence in their lives would soon be changing. His eldest sons were nearly men. Barrett would be going off to school and then university. The notion of rattling around alone held no appeal to him. He'd recently been introduced to a young widow, a woman who might give him more children still. He found the idea of it far more appealing than he'd anticipated.

"Barrett," he called softly. "Come here. I want to see your shooting, Son. Let's see how you've improved."

Dutifully, the boy came to him. He handled the firearm carefully, loading the shot just as instructed numerous times. Under normal circumstances, they'd have had groomsmen or game-keepers with them, but given the conditions, he'd left off with only the four of them. He'd wanted it that way. There were things to discuss that the servants did not need to be party to, after all.

"Very good, Son. Well done, indeed."

Barrett, always so serious, looked up with a rare smile. "Thank you, Father."

Kneeling down, he looked toward a spot on the frozen pond. "I firmly believe that bush, right there at the water's edge, is filled with birds. Filled. I'll send your brothers down to beat the bush and drive them out. You'll do the shooting and I'll do the loading. All right?"

It was a rite of passage and one that Barrett clearly understood as his eyes lit up. "Yes, Papa—I mean, yes, Father."

He smiled down at his son. "I will always be your papa."

Leaving his gun next to Barrett, he walked down to where his eldest sons were wrestling one another into a snow bank. "Go to that bush—quietly—and on my signal, beat it until everything flies out of it. We're going to let Barrett have the first shots this year."

It was Bancroft who laughed. "Like he'll hit anything. He can barely lift the gun!"

"You were small once, too," he reminded his second-born son gently. "He must learn. And he can't do that if he's never given opportunities to try."

Taking the twins' guns and their powder and shot, he trudged back to where Barrett awaited him even as the older boys made their way to the pond's edge. But then the birds took flight, long before they rattled the first branch. They ripped from the frost-draped fronds and soared into the sky with wild cries.

Barrett gamely raised his gun and fired one shot. A single bird fell to the ground. But it wasn't his son's small victory that caught his eye. It was the trio of men exiting the nearby woods. Poachers. Poachers with loaded guns. In his hand, he held two guns and neither of them had a shot in it. Barrett's rifle was spent and his was several feet away from the boy still.

"Well, if it ain't the master of the castle," the first man said.

His speech marked him as a man of London, a man of the streets. What was he doing in northern England? But he kept his reply congenial. "I'm not certain what you're doing here gentlemen, but if you wish to hunt, I'll grant you permission for the day to take what you can carry from the land."

"Oh, we're 'ere to 'unt... but I'm not after birds, your grace. You should 'ave left 'er alone, you know? If you'd just not gone sniffin' round 'er, we wouldn't be 'ere," the man said. Even as he did so, the men beside him raised their guns. "Shame you 'ad to bring all your sons. Who inherits if the lot of you are wiped out?"

He looked at Brendan and Bancroft. They were too far away. All the way by the water's edge with no cover. Any attempt they made to reach safety would only make them better targets. But Barrett, there on the crest of the hill, could duck over the other side and get to the woods.

"Barrett, run! Now!"

Immediately, Barrett did as he asked, but not toward the woods. No. He ran toward the men who had emerged from the woods, brandishing his gun like a club, swinging it with all the might his small body could muster. Lunging forward, he did the same. But it was too late. He felt the pain even before he heard the shot, the scorching heat of it hit him squarely in the gut and then the snow at his feet began to bloom with spots of crimson. Like flower petals on white cloth.

The clamoring and commotion, the screams and shouts of his children echoed on the frozen air. And then two more shots. There wasn't a third, but as his head lolled to one side, he could see Barrett lying in the snow, blood pouring from a gash on his forehead. He'd been struck with the butt of a gun. Even if he survived the wound, the cold would kill him. All of them would die there that day.

Turning his head, unable to look at the sight of his youngest child, at his inability to save him, he turned his face toward the trees and the men fleeing the scene of their crime. And it occurred to him they hadn't been robbed. His watch fob, snuff box and purse remained. The gold buttons on their clothing had not been taken. Those men had come there to kill them all. And then he saw another figure in the trees. It was a face he knew as well as he knew the back of his hand. He simply stood by, waiting for the killers to reach them. Why? But he knew, of course. He knew. It wasn't just the title. It was her.

They would all pay the ultimate price for the pretty widow he'd wanted to spend his old age with.

⟫⟩⟨⟪

"YOUR WAGES, GENTLEMEN," the man who'd hired them said, then passed them a purse heavy with coin. "You've done your jobs. Now, leave at once. It's best if no one sees you in the area. Do not stop until you reach London."

"And you? Your appearance 'ere will be noted," the leader of the band of criminals stated.

"I have the perfect alibi. You need not worry for me," he replied.

"Who is 'e to you? Friend, enemy, rival?" the leader asked.

"Does it matter? You've been paid haven't you?" the gentleman snapped.

The leader smiled. "Right you are, guv'nah. Right you are. Paid well for it."

With that, the gentleman turned on his heel, mounted his horse and rode away.

In the silence that followed, their leader mused, "Only one reason a man wants to kill a duke and all 'is children... that's a title. We'll 'ave a duke in our pockets soon enough, lads."

"Don't seem right... that one don't even 'ave whiskers yet," one of the men said, gesturing back to the clearing where the youngest boy still lay bleeding on the ground. Through the trees, it was just possible to see the halo of pink snow spreading out from his position.

"Don't matter if it's right. Matters we got paid to do the job and do it we did. All that's left is to wait until someone else claims the title.... whether it be the toff that paid us or the toff what paid 'im to do it."

"Then what?" Their third member, and the quietest of them all, asked.

The leader grinned, showing blackened teeth. "Then we keep getting paid for this job. Boys, if we do it right, we'll be kept for life by this one."

"Still don't seem right... just children, Ma—"

"Don't say the name! No names on jobs. Ever. Even if the dead are the only ones to 'ear! 'Sides, it's too bloody late for any guilt now. It's done, ain't it?" the third man replied. "They're all dead and we're the ones what killed them. Don't matter why, does it?"

"It's money." The leader waved the purse in front of the second man's face. "Titles, sure... but all the title does is give you the money. They ain't so different from us. We're all trying to get by, to get more—it's what it's all about. Don't go soft on me. You knew the job fore you ever came out 'ere with us! I'll 'ave your word you'll not breathe about this to another soul or I'll leave another corpse behind to bleed out in the snow."

The second man gave one more glance in direction of the boy—he'd moved. It was no longer just the halo of pink snow. He could now see the boy moving, up on his hands and knees, crawling toward the crest of the hill. He could still die of the vicious blow he'd been dealt. But if the others saw him, they'd go back and finish the job. The only chance he had was for them to get out quickly. Turning back to his compatriots, he shook his head. "I'd never sell you out. Like brothers we are! We're in it together... and that means getting gone from 'ere fore we get caught. London bound, we are. Fast as we can make it."

Heading deeper into the trees, following the path that would lead them back to the road and the hired carriage that awaited them, he dared one glance back. The boy was out of sight now. If he'd offered aid, the others would have killed them both. It was up to fate now, he thought.

Chapter One

October, 1827

G RIFFINGATE WAS HARDLY the sort of palatial ducal estate most expected. Ancient and dark, it bore a greater resemblance to the medieval strongholds of old than to the sort of Palladian grandeur one normally associated with ducal wealth and prestige.

Packed into the small carriage, too small for all of them and their bags, Miss Minerva Stone glanced once more out the window at the imposing structure as they drew near. Had the former dukes intended for it to appear so terribly unwelcoming? She'd heard about the Duke of Hargrieve, of course. Everyone had heard about him. They whispered that he was quite mad. They also whispered that perhaps he had come into the title by means that were quite deliberate and horrifying. She didn't really have any great faith in such gossip. After all, he had been but a child to her understanding when the terrible tragedy that had taken his family's lives had occurred.

Of course, now in the presence of a foreboding manor house, driving along a rutted lane in dismal, overcast weather—the imagination did tend to take flight. Was he mad? Was he a murderer? Had the hellion younger son of her employer, with his propensity for starting fires, sentenced them all to their doom by burning the London townhouse and forcing them to seek refuge at the duke's ancestral home?

A million questions were running through her mind.

"I don't like it."

That pronouncement had come from young Meredith, the only daughter of the Entwhistle-Graves clan and the child she was charged with caring for. There was another child, a boy, who remained in London in the care of a "hospital". Though, Minerva was well aware that was simply another term for asylum. The poor child had been born with some sort of infirmity that his mother would not willingly look upon. He'd been sent away in infancy and was never spoken of by anyone. The elder two sons, seventeen and fifteen respectively, were not expected to be under the charge of a governess.

"I'm certain it's a lovely home. It's only this dismal weather that makes it appear foreboding," Minerva insisted. She wasn't, but as lies went, it was a harmless one.

"Oh, no. It's as vile up close as it appears from a distance," Mrs. Entwhistle-Graves said. Then, as if realizing she should have corrected her daughter, added, "But you must not say such things, Meredith. Your cousin, the duke, has been most kind to open his home to us and allow us to reside here until the house in London can be set to rights. No thanks to your wretched brother, of course."

Minerva managed to keep her eyebrows from arching upward at such a harsh assessment of Peter, the fifteen year old, from his mother. Under normal circumstances, Charlotte Entwhistle-Graves acted as though her children—well her eldest sons, at any rate—were all without fault. They could have beheaded someone, quite literally holding the severed head in their hands, and Mrs. Entwhistle-Graves would have laughed about it and scolded them lightly for making a mess. It was unfathomable to Minerva, but it also wasn't her place to have an opinion about such things and, certainly, it was not her place to express her ideas so freely.

"It's frightening," Meredith insisted. "Don't you think it's frightening, Miss Stone? Filled with ghosts and secret passages!"

Minerva smiled at Meredith's assessment. The child likely hoped for all those things. She always spoke of desperately wanting an adventure. "Oh, not at all. I think it's just a house. Bigger than some and smaller than others, but still just a house for all that. I'm certain once you get there and can explore a little, you'll find you rather like it."

Mrs. Entwhistle-Graves harrumphed, obviously skeptical, before retreating once more to the novel she'd brought to explore during their stops. Stops implied a degree of luxury in travel that they had not experienced.

Minerva had the sneaking suspicion that her employer was not so flush as she had been led to believe. They traveled with only her lady's maid, after all, and two footmen who took turns riding on the back of the carriage for protection. All the other servants had been let go, at least temporarily, following the fire. They'd traveled all the way to Yorkshire with the bare minimum of servants and bags. The boys were crammed into a carriage with whichever footman was off duty. Her employer had declared their boisterous behavior impossible and banished them to ride in the poorly sprung coach that had only ever been intended to hold servants and the most cumbersome of their trunks.

It was not an unusual occurrence. Her employer might extoll her children's virtues to others but she was often at odds with them in private. Save for Willis, the eldest, of course. He was only ever out of favor when Peter was present as Peter could try the patience of a saint. The truth was, Mrs. Charlotte Entwhistle-Graves was the least maternal of mothers she had ever encountered. Half the time, she wasn't even sure the woman recalled her children's names.

"There be ghosts," the maid muttered under her breath in an almost comical wail. "I know it."

Minerva frowned a warning in the woman's direction. There

was no need to fuel Meredith's fantasies of adventure and hauntings. But then, once again, she'd underestimated her charge.

"Are there ghosts, Mama?" the little girl asked in her curiously direct fashion. Naturally, she sounded completely intrigued at the prospect.

"Don't be silly, Meredith. It doesn't suit you. There are no such things as ghosts. Now, do hush all of this nonsense or I will make you ride with your brothers in the other coach," the child's mother said, placing a hand to her head in a dramatic fashion, as if to ward off an impending megrim.

That threat effectively ended all conversation. They rode the rest of the way in silence, the carriage trudging along the rutted and snow-covered lane toward the ominous and foreboding house that would be their new home for the next several months.

Glancing out the window, taking in the dark hulking shape, Minerva found herself wondering if perhaps there weren't ghosts lurking inside.

FROM THE WINDOW of his study, Barrett Falconner Graves, Duke of Hargrieve, watched the approaching carriages with a feeling of dread. It didn't help that he'd consumed a rather alarming amount of brandy the night before and was now paying for his excesses. But it wasn't simply his aching head and rebellious stomach that prompted that emotion. He recognized the lead carriage, after all. He'd paid for it. Purchased it for Charlotte when she'd whined and complained about not having decent transportation for herself and her brood after the death of her husband, his late uncle, Phillip. He'd never held his uncle in any great regard and that sentiment, unfortunately, extended to the vapid and shallow woman the man had married.

Why? What possible purpose did Charlotte have for descending on him with winter approaching? The Season was to start soon, after all, and she'd never been one to miss London and all of its entertainments. No doubt she was up to her eyeballs in debt, he thought bitterly. No matter how generous he was with her, she still overspent. Another niggling fear reared its ugly head. Could it have been something worse? Had she or one of her miscreant sons embroiled themselves in some sort of scandal?

Barrett fervently prayed that was not the case. The family name was besmirched enough with the ludicrous whispers that circulated about his alleged murderous tendencies.

A knock sounded on the door behind him and Hamilton, the long-suffering butler, entered. "Your grace, there are carriages approaching. We are to have guests and the house has not been properly prepared!"

Barrett didn't bother to look back to see if the loyal retainer was wringing his hands. It was the most probable likelihood knowing Hamilton. "I'm aware. Have guest rooms readied as best as possible. If Mrs. Entwhistle-Graves is dissatisfied with the state of her welcome then she will have no one but herself to blame. She should have written that she intended to come for a visit."

The butler offered a deep and most heartfelt sigh that conveyed all his bitter disappointment with the current situation. "Certainly, your grace. I shall see to it. How many children are there?"

"At least a score," Barrett said. "Though they'd be better counted as a legion like the demons they are."

"Pardon, your grace?"

Reminded once more that his butler did not understand sarcasm, Barrett answered flatly, "Three, Hamilton. There are three children. Two boys and a girl... though the boys, I must presume, are all but grown men now, if Charlotte could manage to produce such a creature given that she herself has never managed to behave as anything more than a spoiled child. I'm certain she will have some servants with her, though based on the fact that there are only two carriages, she can't have brought the entire household, at least. Perhaps she doesn't intend to stay long."

The butler's silence was all the answer that was required. Charlotte would stay as long as Charlotte liked. He would simply have to endure.

When the carriages finally reached the small area in front of the low, flat portico at the front of the house, he turned from the window and strode toward the hall. He heard the murmurs outside as Hamilton greeted the uninvited guests. Then they began their invasion, the boys first, Willis and Peter Entwhistle, his step-cousins. Charlotte entered next, her daughter, Meredith—his uncle's only child—behind her. But his gaze was fixed on the woman who entered last.

She was dressed in the most drab garment he'd ever seen, the gray wool intended to make her invisible. But a woman such as she would never be able to escape notice. With her pale blonde hair and vivid green eyes, she was stunningly beautiful. *And also clearly a servant, thus entirely out of his reach.* He'd never been the sort to exploit the powerlessness of a woman in his employee. And if she worked for Charlotte, the sad truth was that she ultimately worked for him as he paid her wages. It was all the more reason to bitterly resent his aunt and her intrusion. She'd robbed him of his peace and quiet and brought a forbidden siren into his home.

"Barrett!" Charlotte called out with false warmth as she approached him. They did not embrace. She kissed the air inches from his cheek and then backed away with a too bright smile. "It's so delightful to be here at Griffingate again."

"It would have been more delightful had I known of your impending arrival. I might have actually had the house in order," he answered coolly and with a distinctive bite to his tone.

The blonde woman who remained close to the little girl—a mark of her position as governess, no doubt—glanced up at that, her gaze narrowing suspiciously in Charlotte's direction. As for Charlotte, her response was a tittering laugh far more suited to the debutante she had once been than the matron she currently was.

"The mail is so terribly unreliable," his aunt offered breezily. "They are so very concerned with how quickly the coaches can get from one town to another that they simply overlook whether the mail they are intended to carry also gets there! And, after all, Barrett, it isn't as if we are guests. We are your family. All the family you have left... such a terrible tragedy it was."

There it was. The twisting of that bitter, poisoned blade in his gut. Charlotte was often keen to remind him that she and his late uncle had taken him in after the death of his father and brothers, that they had fed, clothed and sheltered him despite the rumors, despite the inquest, and despite their own doubts about his innocence. It was something that would be invoked as currency for all of his life, he feared. "Hamilton is having the maids ready your rooms. You will excuse me, Charlotte, but there are some pressing matters I must attend to. Supper will be at six. We keep country hours. It will be simple fare, but plentiful. You will all dine with me tonight."

"Even me?"

Barrett's gaze snapped to the small girl who'd asked the question. She was young. Only eight or so, he guessed. She'd been born long after he'd departed his uncle's home, after he'd returned to Griffingate and begun running his own affairs. In fact, she was the only reason, following his uncle's death, that he continued to support Charlotte. She was the only person with whom he shared a blood connection, even if she was a stranger to him. "What is your name, Child?"

"Meredith, your grace," the little girl replied, then sketched a not quite perfect curtsy.

"Then, yes, Meredith, even you. We shall all dine together... and your governess. We have too few servants to have them traipsing up and down the stairs carting trays to half a dozen chambers," Barrett said, seizing upon the only explanation he had as to why he wished the governess at the dinner table.

Charlotte smiled. "I daresay it will be good for Miss Stone to observe Meredith's table manners in such a setting. What an excellent notion, Nephew! Before your pressing matters take your attention entirely... I do need to discuss something with you. There was a bit of an accident with the London house, you see..."

Chapter Two

H E HADN'T SPOKEN to her. Not a single word that escaped the
perfectly sculpted lips of the Duke of Hargrieve had been
directed at her. And yet, as she stood there in the entryway of his
ancestral home, her kid boots rooted to the floor and her breath
coming in shallow pants, Minerva found herself completely and
utterly bowled over by him.

Why? In all the years she'd heard the rampant gossip about
him, in all the times his name had been mentioned in scandal
sheets dredging up the ancient rumors about the demise of his
father and brothers, had no one ever mentioned his appearance?
They called him mad. They called him a murderer. They called
him a grasping and wicked man. They had never called him
handsome.

But then handsome was hardly an apt description, was it?
Had someone asked her to describe what the God of War had
looked like in her mythology classes at the Darrow School, she
likely would have been unable to do so. But the picture in her
mind that defied words would quite likely have been a very clear
match to the man who had just walked away with her employer.
With his dark hair, chiseled features and flashing eyes—he'd fair
taken her breath. Even his dour and disapproving expression had
not muted his appeal. A man like that could only be described in
one word for a woman in her position—dangerous.

"Mama did not write a letter to the duke, did she?" Meredith asked.

"I think not," Minerva agreed softly. "No doubt, she thought the circumstances surrounding your need for an extended visit would be better taken when explained in person." After all, how did one say they'd burned down a large portion of the family's very expensive and well-appointed London home? There was no good way to share such news.

"She thought he'd say no," Meredith replied, direct as always. "Mother often says it's better not to ask permission."

"The phrase I think is 'it is better to ask forgiveness than permission'. And that's not an advisable method," Minerva stated.

Meredith looked up at her then, her expression hovering somewhere between patronizing and sympathetic. "Miss Stone, that may be what others say but that is not what Mama says. She just says it's best not to ask permission. But then I do not think she's sorry, so forgiveness isn't really necessary, is it?"

Minerva blinked at that. It was true enough, she supposed. Rather than answer, she turned her attention back to the duke as he and Mrs. Entwhistle-Graves exited the room. At the last second, he looked over his shoulder, their eyes locking for just a whisper of a moment. Immediately, she regretted it. Her heart hammered in her chest like a drummer going into battle.

Pasting on a false smile in spite of her jittery nerves and the thousands of butterflies that seemed to be swarming in her stomach, Minerva felt flushed and uncomfortable in his presence. *Nonsense*, her sensible self stated firmly. She could find him handsome as she pleased, but there was no point in being foolish about it. He was a duke, after all, and she was far, far beneath his notice.

Realizing the nature of her thoughts, Minerva straightened her spine. *She did not want his notice.* She was a governess—a very good one. As a graduate of the Darrow School, she was an accomplished woman in her own right and dedicated to the education and care of children in her charge. The notice of a man was not something she desired, nor was it something she aspired to. Handsome duke or otherwise, she would not make a fool of herself for any man nor would she ever permit a man to make a fool of her.

At that moment, a maid emerged from a hidden door in the corridor. "This way, Miss," she said. "I'll show you and the wee one to your rooms."

Meredith's eyes rolled at the pronouncement of her as a "wee one". Rather than see the very grown-up little girl scold the maid to tears, Minerva placed a warning hand on her shoulder. "Miss Meredith and I would very much appreciate that. What is your name?"

"I'm Sally, Miss."

"Stone. Miss Stone. I am Miss Meredith's governess," Minerva explained. "Thank you, Sally."

The maid blushed, smiled sweetly and then made for the stairs, leaving them to fall in behind her. They were steep and somewhat treacherous, those stairs. The stones were worn in crescent-shaped patterns at their centers from what could only be centuries of footsteps. Reaching the upper floors, they moved along the corridor toward a large suite of rooms at the end of the hall. There was a sitting room that would suffice as a schoolroom with two bedchambers that opened off it, one for Meredith and one for herself.

"I had thought I would be staying in the servants' quarters," Minerva said.

"No, Miss. His grace insisted. He said it wouldn't be right for Miss Meredith to be separated from you so much during your visit."

She might have protested. She was a governess, of course, and not a guest or a maid. There would be some concession to her slightly elevated standing based upon that when assigning chambers, typically. Having a chamber of her own was not so unusual, but having one so fine was certainly a bit of a stretch. Of course, there were other reasons to want very much to stay in that room. Being closer to Meredith might provide some sort of protection for her. Since Peter had been expelled from school, his attentions toward her had been rather marked and rather uncomfortable. Having her chamber in such close proximity to his younger sister's might help her to stave off any unwanted visits. She couldn't be entirely certain, but she strongly suspected that the fire had occurred because he had been skulking about in the corridors trying to catch her in a position where he might be able to do something unthinkable.

"Well, that is very thoughtful of him. Thank you, Sally," Minerva managed to utter.

Sally exited the room and she and Meredith were alone.

"The door locks," Meredith pointed out. "But we could share a room. It might be better that way."

Minerva frowned. "What have you heard?"

"You're not the first pretty governess I've had, Miss Stone. I know Peter chased off the last one. And I know he'll try to come for you. He always does. Mother knows and she does nothing to stop him," Meredith replied. "But I don't want you to go. I like you. I didn't like the others."

Minerva's blood ran a bit cold at that. How much had the poor child witnessed? "What did he do to the other governess?"

"He kissed her, but she didn't want to be kissed by him. She cried and then he became very angry and hit her. The next day, Mother sent her away."

Minerva nodded then. "We will stick together, you and I. I will keep him from picking on you and you will keep him from picking on me. All right?"

Meredith nodded. "Yes. I think that is an excellent idea."

"Why are you here, Charlotte?" Barrett demanded as his aunt followed him into his study. Even hungover as he was, he found himself contemplating another drink just to ease the agony of her sudden appearance. Wherever Charlotte went, misery followed.

"The house is ruined," she stated simply, as if it weren't something horrific. She might have been talking about a dress or a single piece of furniture for all the significance she gave it.

"That requires a bit of exposition," he snapped.

Charlotte shrugged. "Fire. There was some sort of accident. Perhaps one of the servants was careless with a candle. But the upper floors of the house are uninhabitable... and with the Season underway, there are no houses available to let that wouldn't see us ruined in other ways. I thought it better to retreat to the country and enjoy a bit of family time than to take an unfashionable address and have all of society gossiping about us... again."

Ignoring the jab and her pointed reminder that he was the reason they were all talked about, he demanded, "The house is destroyed entirely? Are you certain?"

"Well, I'm certainly not a builder, Barrett. I know we could not live there as it is. I've retained an architect to survey the damage and he assured me that he has a wonderful cadre of workers at his disposal to put it all to rights."

"Do you have any notion how much that will cost to repair?"

Another shrug, this time accompanied by a coy smile playing about her lips. "Not yet. But the architect has been instructed to send all correspondence to you here, of course. I should imagine that you've received it already unless perhaps it was mislaid along with my own letter to you."

There was no bloody letter. Charlotte did as she pleased then lied through her teeth about it. "If you wish your children to inherit anything from this estate, Charlotte, you should attempt to refrain from bleeding it dry during my lifetime."

"Really, Barrett! You act as if we are impoverished."

"We are not impoverished, Charlotte, but you cannot spend money endlessly without finding some way to refill the family coffers!"

"So marry. Find yourself an heiress," she challenged. "Oh, but you can't. Because no respectable family would ever permit you to marry their daughter because the whole world thinks you are a murderer. Of course, if you could just tell the truth about what happened that day—"

"I have," Barrett snapped, his teeth clenched tight. "I have told the truth about that day—as best that I can. That is not a scar you wish to pick at, Charlotte. I will see the house repaired for you and your brood. But it will involve taking a firmer hand with the household finances."

"Oh, I can economize in some small way, I'm certain. I suppose I could let one or two of the servants go," she said.

"Not you, Charlotte. You are incapable of economizing. I will take over the running of your household finances, or hire someone who will be better equipped to do the job than you are. You and the children will have all that you need, but by my standards and not yours—there will be no excessive shopping, no elaborate dinners for your friends. There will certainly be no entertaining of any kind. Your monthly budget at the wine merchant will be cut by half, if not more," he warned.

She gaped at him, her mouth opening and closing rather like a landed fish. "You cannot be serious."

"I am perfectly serious," he said. "The other option, of course, would be for you to move into the dower house here. The boys will return to school soon and you and Meredith are certainly welcome to remain here in the countryside."

Charlotte waved her hand dismissively while a tittering laugh erupted from her. "That would never work. Sadly, Peter has been expelled from school and will not be returning. The dower house would be entirely too small for the three of us and Miss Stone. Naturally, Meredith must have a governess. Or do you mean to economize her into unemployment? She's quite pricey. That exclusive Hellion Club everyone always talks about. Bastard daughters of gentlemen rearing the legitimate daughters of them! It's all nonsense really. But if one is to have a governess, it must be a Darrow School governess—anything less is terribly unfashionable these days."

"You could always remarry," Barrett pointed out. "I'm certain there is some wealthy man out there who wouldn't mind a twice-widowed woman. Third time's a charm and whatnot."

She shuddered delicately. "I think not. Men are very demanding, Barrett. And husbands are the absolute worst. No. I shall endeavor to make do under your grossly unfair edicts about maintaining dignity in genteel poverty... for the time being."

Barrett nodded. It was all a sham, of course. Charlotte would never do it. At least not for long. "I really do have a great deal of work to do. If you'll excuse me, Charlotte?"

She nodded. "Certainly. I shall have a bit of a lie down before dinner. Very trying journey. Sharing a carriage with children is dreadful. Avoid it all costs if you can."

He waited until she'd reached the door before asking, "By the way, what did Peter get expelled for?"

She shrugged. "It seems someone set a small fire in the dormitory. Of course, Peter didn't do it, but you know how it is. Someone must always take the blame."

A fire at the dormitory. A fire at the house in Mayfair. And, as always, Charlotte dismissed it out of hand because she refused to accept that her children, or at the very least, her sons, were entirely beyond her control. Devils. They were devils. It wasn't any sort of maternal blindness to their faults, either. It was Charlotte's unwillingness to intervene. It was inconvenient for her. "Well, then it's a good thing nearly everything at Griffingate is made of stone and soaked in centuries worth of damp. Fire would not stand a chance. I will see you at dinner."

Chapter Three

S HE'D CHANGED FROM her drab gray traveling dress to a dinner gown of a deep, midnight blue. It was the finest garment she possessed. Arguably, it was too fine for anyone of her station. Of course, her situation had always been somewhat different from the other girls at the Darrow School. Her father might never publicly acknowledge her, but he was generous with her care. He tried to be. That was probably a more accurate assessment. Minerva rarely allowed him to do the things for her that he wished to. It had seemed terribly unfair to flaunt his generosity in front of her friends when their own fathers offered so little in the way of care or support.

In truth, she had much to be grateful for. She'd never lacked for clothing or creature comforts. Her father had supplied a healthy allowance to her at the Darrow School, one that rendered her employment unnecessary entirely. He'd even offered to have her launched into society. But that was not the life for her. Besides, it wasn't the need for wages that prompted her to work. It had never been her wish to be idle, to rest on the generosity of her father. After all, his legitimate heirs could just as easily take all of that away without warning should he pass. And given her father's advanced age and his degree of dissipation, that eventuality was certainly something that would occur sooner rather than later.

Another glance in the mirror as she tidied her hair and secured a slipping hairpin, then Minerva was stepping into the
shared sitting area to collect Meredith. The little girl was dressed
in yellow—a shade that made her look sickly. But Mrs. Entwhistle-Graves insisted that Meredith always be dressed in colors that
did not suit her. The girl's nearly impossible curls had been pulled
back into thick, tight braids that were painful to even look at. No
doubt, she'd have a headache from it all before the night was
through.

"I take it your mother sent Winchell to do your hair?" Minerva asked.

Meredith nodded, looking positively miserable. "It hurts."

Minerva moved toward the girl, turned her around and loosened the ribbons at the base of the braids. Systematically, she
loosened the too-tight coiffure until the child would at least be
able to sit through dinner without being in pain. "There. Is that
better?"

Meredith sighed in relief. "Ever so much."

"Hopefully, your mother will not notice. Let's head down. If
we're late, there will undoubtedly be consequences," Minerva
posited.

Taking the girl's hand, more for her own peace of mind than
because Meredith felt the need of it, Minerva led her from their
chamber to the stairs. Descending to the main floor, they found
everyone else gathered in the drawing room just off the entryway.

Mrs. Entwhistle-Graves was dressed more as if she intended
to attend a ball than a simple dinner at home with the family. Her
gown was of ruby silk and her hair had been exquisitely curled
while diamonds and pearls swathed her neck.

"There you are," she said. "I had thought we might have to
send someone out in search! Heavens, Miss Stone. As a governess, promptness really should be striven for with more
regularity!"

Minerva bit the inside of her cheek and inclined her head.

When she could speak, she replied, "I shall certainly endeavor to improve, Mrs. Entwhistle-Graves. Thank you."

Peter and Willis, the sons from her employer's first marriage and half-brothers to her charge, stood before the fireplace. They leaned against it in a close facsimile of nonchalance, though there was something about their efforts that smacked of trying too hard. The deceptively casual stance reflected a cultivated air of indifference rather than true indolence. In short, they were attempting to be impressive in the presence of their cousin, the duke, like true Corinthians. But they were failing.

As if the very thought of him directed her gaze, her eyes shifted about the perimeter of the room until they landed upon him. He was standing near the windows, looking out on to the damp, barren landscape. There was something in his posture that hinted at his troubled state of mind. It was almost as if she could sense the weight resting upon his shoulders. It was easy to imagine that Mrs. Entwhistle-Graves would do little to reduce the degree of burden she and her children created in his life.

Another glance in the direction of the brothers and she noted that Peter was eyeing her much like a cat would eye a mouse. It made her skin crawl. How could a fifteen year old manifest such complete menace? Removing them from London and the familiarity of his own home would not curb his improper behavior. Not even the fact that she shared a chamber with Meredith would dissuade him. She'd be locking the door and fixing a chair beneath the knob, she decided. It was the safest course of action.

The gong sounded then. The duke turned and she saw his gaze settle briefly on his male cousins before continuing toward her. There was a slight tightening of his jaw, a hint of anger there. What had prompted it? Was he put out at having to house a governess? Had either Peter or Willis said something about her in his presence that would make him reluctant to have her in his home? It was impossible to guess and she was already quite nervous given the very unusual predicament they were now in, having essentially shown up uninvited and to a very uncertain welcome.

Mrs. Entwhistle-Graves cleared her throat lightly. The tense moment passed and the duke turned to his aunt, offering her his arm as she had clearly expected him to do.

Willis and Peter fell into step behind them and she brought up the rear with Meredith by her side. It was just as well. It made her very nervous to have Peter at her back. Willis was the sort who would take advantage if opportunity presented itself. Peter, however, was another matter entirely. He was the sort who would go to any length necessary to create the opportunity he desired. And since his desire, at least at the moment, was to possess her regardless of her willingness to be had, their new location at a very isolated country estate was far from ideal. The house was more spacious, the servants too few in number to afford the protection of witnesses, and if she ran—well, there was nowhere to go, was there?

AFTER DINNER, THEY'D returned to the drawing room. As Barrett was acutely aware of his cousins' intentions, retreating to his study was out of the question. When he'd entered the drawing room prior to dinner, he'd found Willis and Peter deep in conversation about the pretty governess. *No. Not pretty. Beautiful. Hauntingly so.* Her appearance aside, the greater issue at present were the nefarious plans his young cousin had hatched. He had been correct in his assumption, it seemed, that the fire at the London house had been set by Peter and the fire at the school, as well. But it wasn't simply a fascination with fire or a predilection for mischief that had seen him commit such acts.

The fire at school had been set for the express purpose of getting expelled. The boy had wanted to be at home where Miss Stone was so that he might have unfettered access to her. So what, then, was the purpose of setting the fire at home? It was a conundrum to be certain.

Initially, upon hearing those things in conversation, he'd wondered if perhaps he'd been wrong about the young woman. Perhaps, he'd thought, she welcomed the attentions of Peter. Though she was Meredith's governess, the difference in their ages would not have been so great. She would have been eighteen or nineteen, he thought, to Peter's fifteen. And yet, as the conversation had gone on, he'd realized that Peter wasn't speaking of arranging a tryst without being caught. Instead, he was puzzling out how best to take the governess herself unawares. It didn't take a great deal of imagination to discern the reasons for such an ambush. If Miss Stone welcomed the boy's attentions, he wouldn't need to go to such lengths for a moment alone with her. Further, it seemed that Peter had much more on his mind than simply stealing a kiss from a pretty girl. His intentions were much more wicked and were so far beyond contemptible that Barrett found himself unable to even look at the boy. If he did, his temper would get the better of him.

Quietly furious, he contemplated how best to address the situation as he studiously looked away from the pair. For the sake of Miss Stone's reputation, it would have to be handled with a degree of discretion. Servants, even the best of them, were terrible gossips and the lot of them could be far more judgmental than even the harshest of society matrons. If there was even a hint of impropriety about Miss Stone, they would turn on her in an instant.

So he was left in a quandary of how to protect her without making her a source of gossip. He'd have to stand guard, he realized. In a circumspect fashion, of course, but he would have to set himself to patrol the corridor outside her room. Lurking in the corridor outside her chambers was hardly the best way, but it seemed the only solution, at least until he could catch the boy in the act and take appropriate measures. The first thing he needed to address was the expulsion. But he wouldn't send him back to

Eton. Peter clearly needed a different sort of environment—one where he would get structure, greater supervision and guidance that might, with luck and time, put him on a different path.

Considering the matter, he made a decision. He'd reach out to someone else—to Highcliff. There was a school that would put Peter on the straight and narrow and Highcliff was the man to get him into it. He'd graduated from it himself, after all. None of the other schools would take him.

"She's quite lovely, isn't she?" The question had been posed by Charlotte. She was smiling indulgently at her youngest son.

"Who is?" It was a deliberately obtuse answer. They were both well aware of whom she was speaking.

"Miss Stone, of course. A bastard governess, yes, but a very pretty one. Do not let her turn your head, Cousin. After all, she'd hardly refill the family coffers, would she?"

"You're speaking out of turn, Aunt," he said. "And of things which are none of your concern."

"She's my daughter's governess. Of course, it is my concern. Good governesses are terribly difficult to come by, you know? And, lud, if I ever had to call her your grace—but she's not the sort you'd marry. Only the sort you'd bed."

Barrett cut his eyes in her direction, his expression impossibly cool. "Despite what the gossips might whisper, Aunt, I am a man of honor. Were I not, I'd have left you to freeze on the doorstep when you showed up unannounced and uninvited with your brood in tow."

Charlotte's tinkling laugh was grating, as was the sneer that accompanied it. "Oh, dear. You are quite full of yourself, Barrett. A man of honor. What nonsense. Honor is simply a word men throw about to justify their fits of temper. Little boys playing at war. And you may invoke your honor all you wish, but I've seen the way you cut your eyes in her direction. I've noticed how terribly aware you are of her presence. Honor, indeed. Is it a match for her pretty eyes and winsome smile?"

"Neither the prettiness of her eyes nor the winsomeness of

her smile is of consequence. Honor is about prioritizing what is right above what one desires," Barrett snapped. "It's a concept I do not expect you to have a great deal of familiarity with as you've clearly never curbed your own willful ways and certainly have not interceded when it comes to the willfulness of your progeny."

"Perhaps you are correct, Barrett," she agreed quietly. "Despite having three children, I am not especially maternal. It simply defies my nature. As you appear to be the expert on child rearing and morality, perhaps it would be best if I simply left the children in your care!"

"That is not what I said, Charlotte," he snapped.

Continuing on as if he hadn't spoke at all, Charlotte mused, "Obviously I cannot return to London as I have nowhere to live in that delightful city at present, but I have many friends in Bath at this time of year. An extended stay there, taking the waters and resting my poor mind after the turmoil of the fire might be just what the doctor ordered! How very kind of you to suggest it."

It was at that moment that Barrett realized he'd walked directly into the trap she'd laid. He'd sprung it like a skittish hare and now he was firmly caught.

Chapter Four

B ARRETT WAS STILL fuming, still trying to find some way of foiling Charlotte's plan to foist her offspring on him. But rather than argue with her in front of everyone, he seated himself far enough from her to preclude the necessity of conversation. It gave him full view of the pianoforte in the corner which had been opened. He had not ordered it so. Before he could question it, Charlotte smirked at him victoriously before turning to the governess.

"You'll play for us, Miss Stone," Charlotte said commandingly. It wasn't a question, at all, nor was it asked in what one could call a pleasing manner. Charlotte's tone was cold and biting, brooking no argument.

"Certainly, Ma'am," Miss Stone evenly replied and made her way to the instrument. "Meredith, you will turn the pages for me, won't you?"

"I'd be happy to help, Miss Stone."

That offer had come from Peter. Barrett watched as Miss Stone's steps faltered, her expression growing very uncertain. After a moment, she forced a smile. "Thank you, but no. It's an excellent opportunity for me to provide some additional instruction for Meredith. Her music lessons will no doubt be somewhat scarce in the country."

Her hesitation had been a fearful one. He caught it instantly.

The way her shoulders had stiffened, the clenching of her fists. She was afraid of Peter. Which begged the question of just how forward and how inappropriate his cousin had been with her already. The plans he'd overheard Peter and Willis discussing were clearly not the boy's first attempt to take advantage of the young woman.

Thinking about his acquaintance with his step-cousin, he frowned. It wasn't the first time he'd seen evidence of Peter's cruelty. When Peter had been a very small boy, he'd caught him avidly watching a kitten caught in a trap in the stables. The poor mangled thing had been yowling with pain. Peter had made no attempt to help it and had, in fact, seemed to be strangely fascinated by its obvious agony. The entire scene unnerved him still. And when he'd expressed his concerns to Charlotte, she'd informed him that the boy was fine and that he was overreacting—that the violence of his past had him jumping at shadows. Her answer to every criticism of her children had always been that whomever uttered said criticism was overreacting or bullying them.

His gaze moved to Charlotte once more. She'd turned a sympathetic gaze to Peter, her mouth forming a slight moue of disappointment. It sent shivers down his spine. Did she know? Could she really be encouraging him in his behavior toward a woman in her employ? No, he decided. Not encouraging. Charlotte did as she always did. She ignored anything unpleasant and took the path of least resistance. If Peter wanted the governess, Miss Stone, then Charlotte would not aid him, but she would not bestir herself to hinder him either. She'd appear sympathetic to his plight because it was more convenient to her to be his ally than his enemy.

"You can teach her to play every instrument known to man, it'll never get her married. No one will ever want to marry Meredith. She's too strange. Too odd. Too ugly," Peter stated.

Barrett looked to the little girl who had just been so unfairly maligned. She didn't scream or cry. She simply stared at her older brother with a face that appeared entirely too grown up on one so young. It seemed she'd taken his measure and found him quite lacking.

"You will apologize for that immediately," Barrett snapped. "Further, you will take yourself to your chamber until you can behave in a more reasonable manner."

The boy had the audacity to laugh. "On whose authority?"

"On my authority," Barrett answered levelly. "I dislike bullies. And that's what you are. A bully. You lash out at others to cover your own insecurities and the fact that, inside, you're quaking with doubt and fear. It doesn't make you a man to belittle others, Peter. It certainly doesn't make you the type of person that anyone would willingly look up to. If people do what you say or spend time in your presence, they do so out of fear rather than admiration. Is that really what you want?"

That might have been the end of it had Willis not laughed at his brother's discomfiture. Peter whirled on him, fists flying. The two boys clashed together, falling to the floor as they attempted to pummel one another. In the process, they broke an antique table that was no less than two hundred years old. The small figurine placed upon that table would have been smashed into oblivion were it not for the nimble fingers of Miss Stone who grabbed it up and carefully backed away from the fray, pulling Meredith with her.

Rather than let the two young men destroy the drawing room, Barrett removed a bunch of flowers from a vase positioned by the door and took the murky, cold water collected in the bottom of it and tossed the contents on the squabbling brothers. They broke apart, each sitting up and sputtering.

"If you wish to behave like barbarians, you may do so outside," he snapped. "But what you will both do is remove yourself from this room immediately. I've no tolerance for such abominable behavior."

When the boys trudged out, each one glaring daggers at one another and, alternately, Peter looking back to glare daggers at him, Barrett sighed.

Then Charlotte rose. "Indeed, Nephew, you handle them remarkably well. Just as I suspected. Come along, Meredith. I will take you upstairs and put you to bed. We will leave Miss Stone to ascertain whether or not the pianoforte is adequately tuned to see to your lessons while you're here."

When Charlotte and her daughter had breezed out, Barrett found himself in a locked gaze with Miss Stone. She still clutched the porcelain shepherdess in her arms. "I think you can put her down now. The danger is past."

Minerva was simply staring at him. She'd never seen anyone challenge Peter directly, certainly not challenge both Peter and Willis at the same time. He'd made a grave error in judgment, she thought. The boys fought like the very devil, but he'd given them a common enemy. They were devious, at best, and positively evil at worst.

His words had prompted a frown of confusion at first, but then she glanced down and saw the rescued shepherdess still clutched in her now icy hands. "Oh."

As the table that had once been her home was now de-stroyed, Minerva instead placed the figurine atop the pianoforte. "I won't trouble you with the music then. I shall see to Meredith and inspect the instrument in the morning."

"Actually, could you stay for a moment? I have some ques-tions regarding the children that I think would far better be answered by you than by their mother," he replied. "And given that Charlotte tends to direct the conversation to areas she prefers, her absence will help us stay on course."

"Oh, certainly, your grace," she said. "What is it you wish to know?"

"Please sit, Miss Stone," he said, and gestured to one of the small settees that dotted the room. It was a space he rarely occupied, the drawing room, she realized. If people came to visit him, he no doubt typically saw them in his study as it would be related to business. Friends, visitors, guests—those would be in short supply when a man was rumored to have committed both fratricide and patricide. If ever something would limit one's social calendar, those sorts of accusations would certainly fit the bill. It was little wonder he seemed so ill at ease, his broad shoulders tensing and the muscle working in his jaw as if he literally had the weight of the world pressing in on him.

Pushing such thoughts aside—her keen awareness of him represented just how dangerous he was to her—Minerva moved toward the settee he'd indicated. Perching on the edge of it nervously, she clasped her hands in her lap and waited for him to seat himself as well. She didn't think he would bite, after all. Nor did she think him guilty of all the things others whispered about. But he might sack her. He might send her straight back to London. Part of her wished he would. It wouldn't be her decision to leave Meredith then, and she'd be absolved. As always, that thought was followed by a hot wash of guilt. The little girl had no one. And that was something that she understood all too well.

"Do they fight often?" he asked, returning to the chair he'd occupied prior to the melee.

"The boys? Though, I suppose they are not truly boys, are they? Yes. They both have fearsome tempers and are very quick to anger. Peter does lash out, specifically at anyone he sees as being smaller or weaker than himself. I suspect he has suffered similar treatment at school and that is contributing to his outbursts," she surmised. "Though, to be entirely honest, if I may?"

"Please, that is a rare commodity in any house occupied by Charlotte," he quipped.

"I think Peter, regardless of whatever treatment he may have received at school, has a natural inclination toward cruelty. Were it not for Meredith, and the fact that she has no allies and no one to defend her, I would have departed Mrs. Entwhistle-Graves' employ already. I consider it daily, to be perfectly honest."

"I understand," he said. "And I would not hold you to blame had you decided to do so regardless of young Meredith. And beyond a doubt, schools are notorious for such treatment. Children are cruel and vicious and often left to their own devices in such places. Though I confess to wondering if that is only true of boys' schools. Perhaps your own school, the Darrow School I believe, was different?"

She laughed softly. "The Darrow School is very different, your grace. We are never left to our own devices there. And Effie—Miss Darrow—who is the headmistress, would never permit any student to behave with such casual cruelty to another. It is something she would eradicate with alarming efficiency."

"I see. Is Peter's abuse toward young Meredith always so vicious?"

"Tonight was actually quite light in the overall scheme of things," Minerva admitted reluctantly. "Tonight, his cruelty was limited to simple words. But he has hurt her physically in the past. She fears him... and she's indicated that her previous governesses have left the home because of him—because he harmed them in some way."

"And you, Miss Stone? Has he hurt you?"

Not yet.

Uncomfortable with both the thought and under the weight of his piercing gaze, Minerva looked away. "I am very capable of taking care of myself, your grace. Miss Darrow does not let any young woman leave her school without that young woman knowing how to defend herself against any attack or unwanted advances."

He ducked his head, a soft chuckle escaping him. "I didn't ask if you could defend yourself, Miss Stone. I asked if you'd had to. I will not allow any woman in my household to be abused or exploited. If Peter's behavior becomes unbearable, you will come to me at once. I will have your word on it."

"If something occurs that is—beyond what propriety permits, I will inform you, your grace. But I cannot imagine we will stay too long here in the countryside. Regardless of the condition of the London house, Mrs. Entwhistle-Graves is very much a city dweller. She will not be able to tolerate the isolation for long," Minerva observed.

His only response to her assessment was a noncommittal sound. Then he added, "Be that as it may, under this roof, I will be obeyed and I will not permit some callow youth to terrorize the staff and guests. Even when you return to London, Miss Stone, whatever wages Charlotte grants you, they originate from the coffers that I, as the Duke of Hargrieve, manage. In truth, I am as much your employer as she is."

"Very well, your grace," Minerva agreed. "Now, in the interest of maintaining propriety, I have been alone too long in your company. I must go and find Meredith and get her put to bed properly. Mrs. Entwhistle-Graves will likely be telling her stories that are only fit to cause nightmares."

"Good evening, Miss Stone," he said. "And thank you for your quick defense of my property... and also for taking very good care of a little girl I think is too often ignored or tormented."

Minerva was uncertain how to respond to that, so she simply nodded and then quickly exited the room. She didn't dare dawdle. No doubt, Peter would be lurking somewhere. Finding one of the maids in the corridor, she pled for assistance with a convenient excuse.

"I'm so terribly sorry. I seem to have lost my way. Can you escort me back to my chamber? I fear I'll never find it on my own," Minerva lied with a friendly smile.

"Yes, Miss. Follow me."

And with that, she found safety in numbers until she could closet herself once more behind locked doors.

Chapter Five

M EREDITH'S MORNING LESSONS were done. The child was
napping, an unusual event, but then Mrs. Entwhistle-
Graves had insisted on having tea with the girl and that was
enough to exhaust anyone. So Minerva found herself, strangely,
at loose ends. There was no schoolroom to tidy, no lessons to
plan as most of the things she would use for such activities
remained in the London house reeking of smoke.

The fire was a curious thing, she thought, as she strolled
along the gallery of Griffingate, well concealed from the view of
others by heavy velvet drapes. She wasn't overly worried about
Peter finding her there. He'd as soon scrub floors as look at old
portraits, or so he'd said when invited to visit a museum once.

Still, she found herself glancing over her shoulder to be certain that she wouldn't be taken unawares. Again, she wondered if
it wasn't a mistake to stay with the Entwhistle-Graves clan
instead of heading back to Effie and the comfort and safety of the
Darrow School. Slipping silently through the house like a ghost, it
seemed more and more likely that she should have escaped when
she had the chance rather than coming to the country. It was too
isolated, too remote, and she was too keenly aware of the
attractiveness of the shockingly young and alarmingly fit Duke of
Hargrieve.

As if her thoughts had summoned him, she heard the door

open below, the butler's diffident greeting and then the deep rumbling tones of the duke's voice as he replied. Almost against her will, Minerva moved toward those curtains and parted them just an inch so that she might catch a glimpse of him. He was striding through the entryway in his shirtsleeves and breeches, having already removed his coat that was apparently drenched from the rain. The damp linen of his shirt clung to his chest in a way that made her breath catch. He did not follow the conventions of fashion, at all, but dressed more like a common laborer than a duke.

His steps slowed until he came to a stop in the center of the entryway. Then he looked up.

Meredith felt a moment of panic—almost as if he were looking directly at her. That was impossible, of course. There was no chance that she could have been seen. No one, at that great a distance and from his vantage point below, could have detected her presence. Still, she was careful not to let the curtains sway as she stepped back.

Her pulse was pounding and her breathing was rapid, as if she'd run the length of the gallery and back rather than simply glanced through the curtains at a man who could not have been more out of her reach. Clutching one hand to her chest in an effort to still the erratic beating of her heart, Meredith stepped back abruptly and made for the other end of the gallery as quickly as she could. She felt overwhelmed by the need to flee, the need to hide this terrible and utterly pointless reaction to him.

All her life, she'd wondered what it was to feel that stirring of infatuation, to look at a man and be reduced to a blushing, giggling nuisance. She'd never encountered a single member of the opposite sex who'd affected her that way—until him. They'd barely spoken more than a few words to one another, and he'd given no indication at all that he thought of her as anything more than simply a slightly unwelcome servant in his home.

When she neared that end of the gallery and turned the corner, she immediately began backing in the other direction. Peter and Willis were there, lingering in the corridor while a frightened maid ran off in another direction still. Their gazes swiveled immediately toward her and she knew the instant that Peter saw his opportunity.

Hurrying back along the gallery, she had just rounded the corner when Peter caught up to her. He grabbed her elbow, hauling her backward.

"Why are you always running away from me, Miss Stone?" Peter demanded.

He didn't sound like a boy in that moment. There was nothing boyish about him, in fact. He seemed incredibly threatening, menacing in a way that belied his youth entirely.

"Let go of me, Peter. You're hurting my arm," she said, striving for a tone that hid her fear and conveyed the authority she no longer felt she had.

"I asked you a question," he bit out through clenched teeth, his breath hot and damp against her ear.

And at that moment, the duke reached the top of the stairs. His gaze settled on her face and then his jaw clenched—the muscles so taut it was a wonder they did not snap.

"Is there a problem here, Miss Stone?" he asked in a tone that immediately indicated he was well aware that one existed. "Or should I ask you that question, Peter? Is there a problem?"

Peter's grip on her arm eased just a bit. "No problem. Miss Stone stumbled and I caught her. She's terribly clumsy, you know."

The duke looked at her once more. "How strange. In my short acquaintance with Miss Stone I've found her to be very graceful, indeed. Regardless, I should think she's steady enough on her feet now that there's no further need of your assistance. Let her go, Peter."

Abruptly, Peter did so. It was so sudden and so forceful that she actually stumbled forward a bit, so much so that she found herself caught up in the duke's arms, her body pressed against his in a terribly intimate fashion. Given how he was dressed, or rather undressed, it could not be anything but intimate. And Peter was already gone, having turned on his heel and marched back along the gallery where his brother awaited him.

"I'm so sorry," Meredith murmured as she straightened and moved away from the duke. Was it her imagination or did his arms linger about her for just a moment before she had righted herself fully?

"Are you... that is... you were not injured, Miss Stone?" It was clear from his expression that the duke was not at all fooled by Peter's excuse about her near fall. No one with half a brain would have been.

"I am unharmed," she replied, keeping her answer just as veiled as his question.

"And do you often have these... incidents?"

Minerva looked away from him as she answered carefully. "Not often, but certainly more so than I would like. Knowing my propensity for... clumsiness... I try to be very mindful of where I am walking."

"Perhaps, given your propensity for clumsiness, it might be best if you choose not to walk alone. In the event another incident should occur, you would not be without someone to aid you," he suggested mildly. "Though, as your host, I feel it falls to me to remove any potential hazards from your path, Miss Stone. Please remember that."

Minerva couldn't bring herself to look at him. It was all too humiliating. "I will bear that in mind. I think Meredith should be up from her nap now. I should be going."

"Good day, Miss Stone."

"Your grace." She beat a hasty retreat, too terrified to look behind her as she fled his searching gaze.

BARRETT WATCHED HER go, noting that her steps were far more

hurried than necessary. Was she running away from Peter or from him?

It stood to reason that a governess would have heard the rumors about him. No doubt Charlotte had voiced them at length during their journey to Griffingate. She loved nothing more, after all, than to regale everyone with the notion that he was guilty of both fratricide and patricide. Or potentially guilty. After all, there was no proof. But proof was only needed to hang a man. It took nothing more than whispers to ruin him. Duke or no, people were reluctant to invite him into their midst. They treated him the same way he approached a dog he was uncertain of—with extreme caution and hesitation.

For the most part, he was inured to it. The fact that others viewed him as not just a murderer but a monster was something he had grown almost numb to. And yet it was different. She was different. He did not want Miss Minerva Stone to see him that way. He wanted her to look past the rumor and innuendo. He wanted her to see something in him that he wasn't even certain of himself. His own memory of those events was gone entirely. The only proof he had that he was not the one who had murdered his entire family was the fact that he inwardly recoiled at the very thought of it. In the end, that was not very much.

Cursing himself, cursing the fact that he was mooning over a pretty governess he had no business even having an awareness of, he turned to the other problem. Peter. He'd have to do something about the boy and the threat that he posed to the female staff in the household. Making a note to speak to the butler about having the maids work in pairs, he headed for his own chamber to change out of his damp clothes.

The storm that had come up while he'd been riding had been swift and sudden. It had also been welcome. Thoughts of Miss Stone had created a fever in his blood and he'd thought the rain would cure of him his heated thoughts. Little did he know he'd run directly into her upon his return. Of all the damnable luck.

Chapter Six

ON THE THIRD morning of her stay at Griffingate, Minerva awoke to utter chaos. Meredith, normally so stoic and very adult in her demeanor, was sobbing brokenly in the sitting room beyond her door and a maid was all but shrieking her name in alarm.

It was upsetting for Meredith to cry. The child was terribly pragmatic and quite unusual in the way she viewed the world. Such emotional outbursts from her were very few and far between. For something to have overset her so desperately, it must have been truly awful.

Slipping her wrapper on over her shoulders, she tied it firmly at her waist and stepped out into the sitting room to see Meredith on the floor, her head resting on her arms and her small body wracked with great, heaving sobs. There was a piece of paper on the floor beside her. Stooping to retrieve the note, Minerva read it.

At first, she simply couldn't take it in. It was so confounding that she read it a total of three times before she could fully comprehend the contents. Mrs. Entwhistle-Graves was gone. She'd left them. Abandoned the lot of them on the mercy of the duke.

She was not unconcerned about Meredith's heartbreak over the turn of events, but her more pressing concern was that Peter now had even fewer adult eyes on him to curb his wicked behavior. Her second concern was that she was now an unmarried woman in a bachelor household. She was outnumbered and in far over her head.

"She's gone, Miss Stone," Meredith sobbed. "Mother has left us. We're orphans... or as good as."

"I know she is. But not forever... not permanently. You most certainly are not orphaned," Minerva protested, striving for a comforting tone. "She's taken a short sojourn to Bath and will return to collect you very soon, I'm sure."

In fact, she was anything but sure. It was quite possible that Mrs. Charlotte Entwhistle-Graves had no intention of returning for her children. A less maternally inclined person she'd never encountered. For Willis, it would be a simple thing. He'd go back to university after the break and it would have no impact on him at all. As for Peter, well, a school would have to be found that would be willing to take him on and given how many times he had been expelled from every reputable educational establishment, that could take a not insubstantial effort. But for poor Meredith, it would change everything.

Mrs. Entwhistle-Graves was hardly the sort of doting mother who lavished attention or praise on her only daughter. In fact, more often than not, she was terribly critical of Meredith. But Meredith was accustomed to her—to her criticisms, yes, but more specifically to her presence. The little girl was heartbroken at what she saw as her mother's abandonment and, in truth, Minerva couldn't blame her for it. The woman had slipped away like a thief in the night because it was more convenient for her to do so than to deal with her children's messy goodbyes. Her home in a shambles, forced to live in a new and unfamiliar place with someone she knew not at all being in charge of her, namely the duke, and now her own mother abandoning her—it was too much. No wonder she was so terribly overset.

"She won't come back," Meredith said. The little girl sat up then, swiping angrily at her tears. "She'll write us letters and tell us she misses us for a week or so. And then those letters will come less and less often and, eventually, she won't write us anymore at all. It's her way. The duke won't want us here... not when Peter causes ever so much trouble. And I'm just a girl—no one ever has any use for us."

Out of the mouths of babes.

"I'll get dressed and go down to speak with the duke over breakfast. Perhaps, we can come up with some sort of solution. In the meantime, you should go rest and put a cold, damp cloth over your eyes. Otherwise, all those tears will give you a terrible headache," Minerva offered gently.

Meredith nodded and climbed up from the floor. She looked impossibly small, frail and despondent. In short, she looked like the orphan she felt herself to be in that moment.

Impulsively, Minerva leaned in and kissed the top of the girl's head—a gesture of affection and reassurance that was much needed by both of them. When Meredith had gone back to her bed, Minerva made quick work of donning her drab, gray day dress. Her hair was still braided from the night, so she simply pinned it up in a simple coil before leaving their chamber to find the duke. It wasn't difficult. He was, she had learned, a creature of habit. As per the normal morning routine, he was in the breakfast room, enjoying a hearty meal before he began his daily work.

"Your grace," she said, dropping into a curtsy as she entered. "I'm afraid there is a bit of a catastrophe at hand."

"Charlotte's departure?" he asked, lifting his cup to his lips. His tone indicated that he was less than pleased with his aunt's behavior. "I had known she planned to leave, but she had guarded the time of her departure as carefully as any state secret. I was quite stunned upon rising to be informed that she had left before daybreak."

"Well, yes. Had she given any indication of her intent to leave the children here?" Minerva asked.

He tossed his serviette onto the table in a gesture of irritation. "She'd said as much, but there had been no time set for her departure, or if there had, she had not disclosed it to me. I had hoped to have an opportunity to change her mind. Sadly, that was not to be. Naturally, the children will remain here. Every necessary measure will be taken for their care and comfort, Miss Stone. You cannot doubt that."

Minerva realized in that moment that he was offended, that somehow, he thought she was insinuating that he would not be a responsible de facto guardian. "Your grace, if I may speak freely?"

"Miss Stone, I cannot imagine that you require permission to do so," he replied tersely. It seemed Meredith was not the only one overset at the turn of events.

"My concern has little to do with your intent to see to the children's comfort. You are an honorable man, I know."

His dark brows rose skeptically. "Do you know it? What a wonder you are, Miss Stone, when every other person thinks me the worst sort of villain!"

"Gossip and rumor very rarely hold more than the merest grain of truth," she replied dismissively. "It is quite apparent after being in your presence for even a short time that the horrible deeds that have been attributed to you are simply not in your nature. But your reputation, your grace, is hardly the concern here. There are much more pressing matters that need to be addressed immediately."

"Go on," he said.

"My concern is for the children and how their mother's abandonment might impact already *frayed tempers*. Willis will be fine, of course. Peter is another matter. A proper school will need to be found for him. But because of his past disciplinary problems, that may be easier said than done. For a variety of reasons, of which you are aware, I cannot provide any instruction for him."

He nodded coolly. "The subject of what to do about Peter has been pressing on me from day one and I do have a solution. I have a school for Peter in mind. I've already sent inquiries. And it is a school that is particularly suited to young men with temperaments such as Peter's. It will be the making of him, Miss Stone, if anything could be."

Relief washed through her at that thought. With Peter taken out of the equation, she could deal with Willis if need be. And Meredith, well, so long as she and the little girl could remain together, they would both be fine. "And Meredith? Will you send her to a school if her mother fails to return? We both know that is a possibility. In fact, I think, in retrospect, given how blasé Mrs. Entwhistle-Graves was about the fire, that she saw it as a perfect opportunity to foist her children upon someone else. It makes me wonder if, in fact, Peter was truly the culprit in that instance."

BARRETT FOLDED THE news sheet and set it aside. He was in a foul mood. It had been a long and mostly sleepless night. Vividly erotic dreams of the very respectable young woman before him had robbed him of any true rest. Being greeted by the news of Charlotte's departure and the ramifications of it had only worsened his already foul mood. "You might as well join me for breakfast, Miss Stone. Apparently we have more to discuss than I had realized."

It goaded him to admit it, but she was correct. Had he been a man above reproach—which he was not—having a governess living in his home with children who were now apparently his wards would not have been such a problem. That said governess was also young and incredibly beautiful would only make the gossip worse. Even avoiding London had not helped him to stay out of the gossip rags. His every move was remarked upon. If he went for an unusually long ride, then he was warring with inner demons. If he attended church, he was seeking absolution. If he failed to attend church, he was a conscienceless murderer incapable of remorse. There was little doubt that news of Miss Stone's presence in his household would get back to those gossipmongering fiends in record time. And as nothing traveled faster than gossip, it would reach London sooner rather than later.

"I have an elderly great-aunt—well, she was married to my grandfather's brother who has long since shuffled off the mortal coil—she lives a short distance away. I will call on her today to fetch her back here so that she might serve as a sort of chaperone," he offered. "It's a nod to propriety, but to be perfectly honest, she's as addled as they come."

"Is it her age?"

"No, Miss Stone. She was always addled. Age simply hasn't helped," he replied caustically. "At this rate, if I keep adding to the number of people living in this house, I'll need to hire more servants."

"Thank you, your grace. In truth, I think being here could be very good for Meredith... but it might be nice if you spent a bit of time with her so that she doesn't feel that she is a burden and is actually welcome."

She was a burden. They were all burdens. But he nodded anyway. There was no point in behaving like an ogre and making a small child miserable simply because he preferred the peace and solitude of his bachelor existence. "Certainly. I will speak to her when I return. In the meantime, I suggest that you take Meredith for a long walk in the company of at least two footmen. I would not leave you in the house unsupervised with Peter. Or Willis for that matter. They are both too used to never being told no for any reason... by anyone."

"That is a rather excellent notion, your grace... though I must ask what you intend to do about the other child?"

"What other child?"

Miss Stone's eyebrows lifted in shock and her full, luscious and perfectly shaped lips parted in shock. The expression should have been comical rather than carnal, and yet everything about her seemed to stir his long repressed libidinous urges. The sooner he could put distance between the two of them the better they would all be.

"Mrs. Entwhistle-Graves' youngest son. She never spoke of him and I believe that she forbade the other children from speaking of him, either. But I had assumed you knew."

Barrett shook his head. "I assure you, I most certainly did not. Where is this child?"

"I am not certain, except to say that he is housed at an institution in London."

Barrett knew all about the institutions his aunt utilized. She'd put him in one for a time, insisting that the head injury he'd received when his entire family had been murdered had left him addled. Only the intercedence by Lord Highcliff, a friend to his eldest brother, had saved him from that wretched fate. Recalling the torment of that place, he suppressed a shudder. "Bedlam?"

Miss Stone looked away, her expression tight and terribly uncomfortable. "I would presume so, your grace. I have no notion what sort of infirmity may be inflicting the child. In truth, I would not have known at all about his existence had a person from the institution not come to collect payment from Mrs. Entwhistle-Graves. Apparently she had failed to make the necessary reimbursements for his care—and they were about to send him to the almshouse if she did not immediately see to the matter. There were raised voices. I wasn't eavesdropping."

"Miss Stone, the child's name?"

"I do not know it, your grace. He was only ever referred to as 'the child' and 'he'. Peter and Willis have never spoken of him and, well, Meredith is so young, I'm not sure how much she actually knows."

"Meredith may not be aware, given her age... but no doubt Willis and Peter would have all the pertinent information. I shall speak with them, but that is no guarantee they will be cooperative. In the meantime, Miss Stone, I have changed my mind about the long walk. You and Meredith shall go with me to my great-aunt's home. I must apparently depart for London immediately and it will be safer for the two of you to remain with her at her home than here. We will ride in an open carriage, well dressed against the cold, and the two of you shall remain there until I return," he said. "I'll not leave any relative of mine to suffer such a fate as that they would inflict in Bedlam."

Miss Stone sighed in relief. "I am very glad to hear it, your grace. I cannot imagine a child suffering in such a place. I have never been, but I have heard horror stories of what it is like."

"It is a horror, Miss Stone. I can assure you of that. Go and make yourself ready. Dress warmly and be certain that Meredith is well bundled against the cold. By carriage, it will take about two hours to reach my great-aunt's home."

Miss Stone rose to her feet. "Thank you, your grace. I will go and see to Meredith now. If it's just the same, I'll ask the cook to have some food bundled for the journey rather than breaking our fast here. The sooner we can depart the better."

He nodded then sat for a moment to watch her go. Her posture would have been the envy of any general. Shoulders squared, spine straight, and her movements, unlike the few young women of his acquaintance, were not dainty or mincing. She strode from the room with purpose and an innate dignity that he found as entrancing as he did admirable. She had invaded his dreams and now she was occupying far more of his waking thoughts than was good for either of them. And there was no time for him to indulge his fascination with her, regardless of the foolishness of it. There was too much to be done.

Rising to his feet, he left his breakfast and made for his own suite of rooms to repair. He missed the two figures lurking in the hall entirely along with the fact that they'd overheard every word.

"He's taking her somewhere else," Peter whispered hotly, his hands clenched into fists. "Mother said I could have her!"

"And you will," Willis replied, knowing how urgent it was to keep Peter's temper in check. Hot-headed as his brother was, he'd likely give the whole plan away. "It's just a delay. Once we get rid of him as mother asked, then she will bring our idiot brother home to claim the title for him and we'll be managing all the accumulated wealth and estates of the Duke of Hargrieve in his stead. Not only will you have her completely at your whim, you will have eliminated the only person who stands in your way."

"We should just shoot him."

"It must look like an accident," Willis cautioned him. "And there is no better time for an accident than on the road. No one will suspect a thing."

Peter nodded. "Fine. But I want to be the one who does it. He needs to pay for the way he spoke to me."

"Fine. Whatever you require," Willis said. He'd already made peace with the fact that he would one day have to eliminate Peter. He loved his brother, but if there was one thing he understood, it was that their mother had put the wrong child in Bedlam. Of course, John wasn't there because he needed to be. She'd needed to hide him so that Cousin Barrett wouldn't suspect her true motivations. If he'd thought for one second that Charlotte had a chance to get anywhere near the title, he'd never have let them in his home.

Chapter Seven

J UST UNDER AN hour later, they were departing. The barouche, as promised, had been opened to the elements. It was cold, but not unbearably so. With her heavy cloak, a muff, and her warmest gown underneath, Minerva was quite comfortable. Meredith was also dressed in her heaviest layers. The promise of an outing had helped to elevate the child's mood, taking her out of the doldrums that her mother's departure had created. For her part, Minerva was reluctant to mention the reason for the duke's hasty departure to London. She wasn't aware of how just much Meredith knew. The duke, however, was not inclined to mince words.

"Meredith, are Willis and Peter your only siblings?"

"No, your grace," Meredith replied.

"Barrett. We are cousins, Meredith, and you should call me Barrett," he replied evenly. "Your other sibling?"

"We are not permitted to speak of him," the little girl replied. "Mother forbade it."

"Well, not to be cruel in stating the obvious, but your mother is not here. She has, for better or worse, left you in my charge. And I would have you speak of it," he said bluntly.

The little girl was quiet for a moment, chewing the inside of her lip in consternation as she considered his request. Finally, she said, "His name is John. John William Graves. And mother put him in the Bethlem Hospital when he was three years old and I was six. I can't remember very much about him except that he didn't talk. He never spoke a word."

"I see. Thank you, Meredith. I mean to leave you and Miss Stone with a female relation for a very brief time while I head to London to collect your brother and bring him home to Griff-ingate," the duke explained. "I cannot leave him in that *hospital* any longer."

There was silence for a moment. No one spoke. And then without warning, Meredith rose from the bench seat and launched herself at her cousin. She wrapped her arms about the duke's waist and hugged him fiercely.

"Thank you, Cousin Barrett," Meredith whispered softly. Only the shaking of her slight shoulders revealed her tears as her face was pressed firmly against the duke's broad chest.

After a moment of hesitation, clearly confused by the girl's emotional outburst, the duke raised one hand and placed it on the child's back, hugging her back in a fashion that illustrated just how little affection he had received in life. Blinking back tears of her own, Minerva looked away, fixing her gaze on the winter landscape beyond the hedgerows at the side of the road. Whatever else happened, she was convinced beyond anything else, that Mrs. Entwhistle-Graves had underestimated how seriously the duke would take his responsibilities for the children left in his care. She had also underestimated what the potential consequences of her actions might be.

When Meredith returned to her seat, silence settled in the barouche. Only the rhythmic rise and fall of horses' hooves and the bumping of carriage wheels could be heard. But it wasn't an uncomfortable silence. And that, above all else, worried Minerva. If one could be comfortable in silence with a person, that was a telling thing, indeed.

After a long while, Meredith slipped her hand inside the muff Minerva was using. Without hesitation, Minerva enclosed the child's gloved hand in hers.

Meredith leaned over and whispered with all the subtlety and quiet of a charging elephant, "I'm glad Mama left us if it means John can leave that terrible place... and I think I like my cousin."

Minerva smiled. "I think you're very wise, Meredith... and an excellent judge of character."

"I hope Mama doesn't come back. Is that very wicked of me?"

"I don't think it's wicked," Minerva offered reassuringly. "You love your Mama, but loving someone and liking them are not always the same thing. Sometimes, even people who love one another are better off when they are far apart."

BARRETT PRETENDED NOT to overhear the conversation. Meredith obviously hadn't wanted him to. But when Miss Stone met his gaze over Meredith's head, he knew that she was aware. He also knew that there was a warning in her words. It wasn't about love. It was about attraction. Whatever his feelings for her, they could not be acted upon. Remaining far apart was their best option, or as far apart as they could remain in their current circumstances.

Regardless of his firm decision not to act on his attraction to her, he didn't mistake the fact that he was not alone in that feeling. No matter how proper her behavior, it seemed that Miss Stone was as keenly aware of him as he was of her.

The remainder of the drive to his great-aunt's home was mundane. There were no great epiphanies regarding Charlotte's motivations, nor were there any more revelations about the family as a whole. Miss Stone would speak quietly with Meredith when warranted but, otherwise, silence reigned.

When they reached Rossington Manor, his great-aunt's home, he was glad to finally be free of Miss Stone's presence and the temptation she afforded. Disembarking from the barouche, he helped Miss Stone down and then simply scooped Meredith up and placed her feet on the ground. Together, they approached the front door of the manor house which was instantly opened by a long-serving and trusted butler.

"Good day, your grace. Mrs. Whitmore is in the drawing room," the ancient servant informed him.

"Thank you, Simpson," Barrett replied. "I know the way. Miss Stone and Miss Meredith have bags in the barouche. They will be staying with my great-aunt for a few days."

"Certainly, your grace. I'll have them collected and have rooms readied," the butler replied. If he found the sudden intrusion to be inconvenient, his manner would never have given it away.

Striding toward the drawing room, Meredith and Miss Stone in his wake, Barrett opened the pocket doors to the room and found his great-aunt having a conversation with no one. "Great-aunt Sissy, who are you speaking to?"

"Barrett!" she cried, rising from her seated position to close the distance between them. "I was talking to your great-uncle, my long departed husband, of course."

Barrett blinked. Without allowing his concern to enter his voice, he asked, "Is he here?"

"Only in spirit, dear," she answered, enfolding him in an embrace. "You know he's been dead for ages."

"Just making certain that you know it as well," he replied, tolerating the hug as good-naturedly as possible.

"What are you doing here, dear boy? And who have you brought with you? Oh, don't say you've taken a wife! I'd certainly be thrilled if you had, but without a wedding! How I despise elopements when they deprive me of the joy of attending such events!"

Sissy was off and running. She'd abruptly disentangled herself from the effusive embrace she'd greeted him with and was now pacing and wringing her hands as she muttered about orange blossoms. "I am not married, Sissy," Barrett stated.

She beamed at him. "Oh, perfect! There's still time to plan everything."

"No, Sissy. Miss Stone is not my betrothed," he replied. Saying it felt wrong.

"Well, then ask her, Barrett! Good heavens! Girls who look like that don't grow on trees, you know!"

That was the point in which Barrett became entirely flummoxed. It wasn't an unusual occurrence with Sissy. She often left him shaking his head after listening to her talk in circles.

"Mrs. Whitmore, may I present my charge, Miss Meredith Graves?" Miss Stone said softly. "I am her governess, employed by Mrs. Charlotte Entwhistle-Graves. We've recently come to Griffingate to stay while necessary repairs are being made to the London house."

Sissy halted her pacing. "Governess?" She looked to Barrett. "She's a governess?"

"Yes, Great-aunt Sissy. Miss Stone is, by all accounts, an excellent governess," he replied.

"Where is Charlotte now?"

"Bath, I think," Barrett replied.

Sissy turned to Meredith then, eyeing the child curiously. "Left you then, has she?"

Meredith was quiet for a moment, then nodded. "So it would seem, Mrs. Whitmore."

"Call me Aunt Sissy," Mrs. Whitmore replied. "You come sit down here with me on the settee. You, Miss Stone, can take the chair just there, out of earshot. That will allow me to speak to young Meredith and determine if you are the excellent governess my nephew claims."

"Yes, Mrs. Whitmore," Miss Stone replied demurely.

Realizing it was his only opportunity, Barrett stated, "Well, I'm off for London. I shall collect the pair of you on my return. In the meantime, Sissy will see to your comfort."

Alone with Sissy, Minerva smiled uncomfortably. "Thank you so much for your hospitality, Mrs.—that is, Aunt Sissy. It's very kind of you to take us in on such short notice."

Sissy waved her hand dismissively. "Nonsense! I'm alone so

much in this rambling old house. That's why I talk to my dead husband. There's no one else about besides the servants and they all look dreadfully uncomfortable when I try to have conversations with them... as if they're about to be called on the carpet."

Minerva's smile relaxed. Lonely, she thought. Sissy was lonely in that big house alone. It was something that she certainly understood. Even in the crowded corridors of the Darrow School, she'd often felt alone. "Wouldn't it be better to talk to someone who answered back?"

"Oh, heavens no!" Sissy said. "We were married for thirty years and he hardly ever answered more than a grunt. It's no different now, is it? Now, have a seat yon, while Meredith and I have a conversation. Child?"

Meredith stopped gawking at a portrait of a nude woman hanging on the wall that was surely more suited to a house of ill repute than a country manor. "Yes, Aunt Sissy?"

Mrs. Whitmore patted the settee next to her, while Minerva seated herself as far from that point as possible without leaving the room. Meredith reluctantly approached and took a seat next to the elderly woman.

"Tell me, Child, is your governess a nice lady?"

Minerva looked away. There was no chance of not overhearing every word of the conversation but she would dutifully pretend not to if it was required.

"The very nicest, Aunt Sissy. I like her very much."

"And your cousin, the duke... do you like him?"

"Yes, Ma'am," Meredith answered. "He seems very nice, as well."

"Do you think they like one another?" Mrs. Whitmore asked with all the subtlety of a cannon shot.

Meredith glanced over at her, a coy smile playing about her lips. Minerva shook her head, but Meredith simply looked back at Sissy and nodded in the affirmative. "I think they do. Very much so. But they try to act like they don't. They're always looking at one another whenever we are all in the same room."

Mrs. Whitmore hummed with pleasure. "I thought so. I have a sense about these things. Now, you run along. If you go out that door and to the left, there's a long corridor. There is nothing in it that can be broken from one end to the other. The floors have also been recently polished. I imagine that if you take off at a run at one end, from about halfway down, you can slide in your stockinged feet all the way to the other end. It's quite fun. I haven't done it in ages, of course. Old, fragile bones be damned."

Immediately, Meredith was taking off her shoes and, for the first time since Minerva had known her, she actually looked like a child. So in that instance, Minerva did not correct her. Nor did she caution her about being a lady or maintaining decorum. There was enough time for all that when Meredith was grown, she thought. The girl ought to be a child while she could.

When she had gone, Sissy patted the settee beside her just vacated by Meredith. "Sit down, Miss Stone. I have questions for you."

Assuming that Aunt Sissy simply wanted to get to know her, Minerva did as she'd been bade. "What would you like to know, Mrs. Whitmore?"

"Aunt Sissy," she said. "That directive was not only for young Meredith. I dislike such formality. Now, are you in love with my nephew?"

Minerva blinked rapidly, taken aback by such a direct question. Finally, after a moment, she managed, "I hardly know him, Aunt Sissy. And even if I did know him well enough to form such an attachment, it would hardly be advisable. I am a governess, after all, and he is—well, he is of a station where he must marry accordingly. It would be pointless to indulge any emotional attachment to him."

"Pish posh! That boy will not marry any wilting society miss," Sissy said dismissively. "After what he's endured in life, they'd bore him to tears. He needs a woman of substance. A woman who understands what strife and disappointment are so that she can truly be there for him. A woman of passion, Miss Stone!

That's what my nephew needs."

"I know he suffered terrible losses at a tender age—" Minerva began.

"Oh, that's not it at all! I mean, yes, it was terrible," Sissy replied, "but it's what that wretch Charlotte did to him after! The boy had nearly been brained with the butt of a firearm and they kept demanding he remember that he had murdered his father and brothers. It was a wonder he could remember his name! So she locked him up. Put him in Bedlam like he was some sort of lunatic."

Minerva instantly recalled the look of horror that had crossed the duke's face when he'd been informed of the fate of Mrs. Entwhistle-Graves' youngest child. The resolve that he'd expressed in stating that it would not continue made perfect sense to her in that moment. It wasn't the injustice of it which had motivated him so much of his own memories of the torment such a place could inflict upon a child.

Minerva's voice quaked just a bit when she asked, "How long was he there?"

"Nearly a year," Sissy stated. "I had begged and pleaded for Charlotte and Phillip to have him released and they simply would have none of it. So I went over their heads and wrote to Lord Highcliff."

"Highcliff?" Minerva jumped at the very familiar name.

"Yes. Highcliff had been a friend to Brendan, Barrett's oldest brother. School chums. He provided invaluable assistance, though I imagine it came with some cost," Sissy stated. "You know him? Highcliff?"

"I know of him. I am a graduate of the Darrow School."

"Ah... Miss Euphemia Darrow. I should have known. I knew her father quite well. To his credit, he never denied his daughter, though I cannot say that has made her life any easier. I always suspected Highcliff had some tendre for her."

"I've often suspected the same... and that it is returned," Minerva replied. It was a thoughtless reply and one that she ought to have felt guilty about. Gossiping about Effie was hardly the way to repay her for all the kindness and care.

Sissy grinned. "Well, if you will not let me play matchmaker for you and my nephew, then I shall play matchmaker for those two misguided fools. There is nothing to say, Miss Stone— Minerva—that we cannot take young Meredith to London ourselves."

Minerva ought to protest. But when she thought of how miserable Effie had been for the past several months, she found herself nodding. "You are quite right, Aunt Sissy. Sometimes, people simply need a push in the right direction... especially when they allow pride to stand in their way."

Sissy's smile took on a calculating quality. "I could not agree more. But first, we have to see you outfitted in something better than these terribly drab colors. My heavens! Did Charlotte do that to you?"

"No. As a governess, it rather behooves one to blend into the wallpaper," Minerva replied. "Attracting attention to oneself can be grounds for dismissal, but also, it can put one in untenable situations with the male members of the household."

"Ah," Sissy said. "I see. Well, your attempts to make yourself plain, Child, are a dismal failure. One might as well tell the sun not to shine or the rain not to fall. Forget all of that nonsense. We will get you sorted out."

Chapter Eight

SIX DAYS. IT had taken him six days to reach London. Frustrated, tired, muddy and at the end of his patience, he'd booked a set of rooms at Mivart's. It was a nuisance to stay in a hotel when he had a house in London, but until the fire damage could be assessed to his liking it, would have to do.

The travel delays had been the result of a series of misadventures. A broken carriage wheel. A lame horse. A washed-out bridge. A fallen tree in the roadway. Every possible delay. Every possible disaster. What should have taken no more than three days had taken what seemed to be ages.

Dirty, mud-splattered, tired and hungry, he waited for the hotel's discreet and impeccable staff to ready a bath for him. Once he was clean, then he would see about the matters which had initially brought him to town. He needed to discern how much damage had been done to the house and whether or not it could, for a reasonable sum, be rendered habitable again. Then he needed to retrieve his young cousin from the hellhole that was Bedlam. He could hardly bring the child to Mivart's. Even if the child had been perfectly sane before entering that hellhole, he likely would not be so coming out of it. He would need a quiet place to recuperate, hence the issue of the house and whatever disaster awaited him there.

Placing a hand at the back of his neck, Barrett kneaded the

sore and aching muscles there. He was beyond tired. It didn't help that regardless of the degree of comfort at any available coaching inn along the way, his nights had been restless. The blame for that could be laid squarely at the feet of Miss Minerva Stone. Never in his life had a woman affected him so. He could not remove her from his mind, no matter what he tried.

The image of her plagued him relentlessly. But not the image of her as she was—prim and buttoned up. No, indeed. His imagination and his long-suppressed desires for female companionship had taken more than liberal license with his memories of her. Half-naked, reclining in his bed with a spill of golden hair about her with her rosy lips parted in invitation. Every image of her was more carnal and more tempting than the last. If he did manage to succumb to sleep, she invaded his dreams. It was an endless cycle of torment.

"Your bath is prepared, your grace," one of the servants informed him.

Turning, realizing that the young man had been speaking for some time and he'd been utterly lost in his own thoughts, Barrett shook his head. "That will be all."

The servant nodded and, as all good servants managed, disappeared quietly. Alone, Barrett stripped off his soiled clothing. He had no valet. As a man who rarely entered society, who rarely socialized at all, he'd never felt the need to fuss with his appearance. Whether in town or roaming the countryside in his shirtsleeves, it hardly mattered. He preferred to keep things simple.

Once he'd divested himself of his dirty clothes, he sank into the tub of hot water and groaned at the sensation. He hadn't realized how tired and sore he was from days on end of bouncing in the damned carriage. But then his stomach rumbled and he knew the bath would have to be short-lived. He was starving, as well.

Washing the dirt and grime from himself, he found his thoughts once more drifting to Miss Stone. It would be easy enough to imagine that it was her hands sliding over his skin, that she was touching him for purposes beyond the perfunctory notion of cleanliness. But he didn't want that. He didn't want some sad imitation of her touch, some hollow fantasy that would leave him disappointed in the end. Because while he wanted her desperately, it wasn't simply the physical release of intercourse that he craved. He wanted to touch her intimately, but also affectionately. He wanted to hold her in his arms while they both slept. In short, he was on a dangerous and slippery slope that went far beyond attraction and, instead, led to the quagmire of infatuation.

She represented a complication. And he didn't need complications in his life. Nor did he need the gossip and questions that would follow if he were to marry.

Cursing Miss Stone, himself, his aunt for bringing her to his door and every other blessed thing that presented a temptation and a complication in his life, he closed his eyes and wished it all to perdition.

THE HOUSE IN Mayfair that Sissy took them to belonged to a friend of hers who was currently on the Continent. It was lovely—appointed with luxurious furnishings, beautiful artwork and all manner of items that were simply beyond price.

"It's like the museum you took me to," Meredith mused.

"It rather is," Minerva agreed as they took their seats in the drawing room.

"Now," Sissy said, ignoring their awed whispers, "the dressmaker shall arrive shortly. I sent instructions that she should bring items that we can alter to fit you immediately. She shall be well compensated for her efforts."

"Aunt Sissy, I cannot permit you to purchase a new wardrobe for me," Minerva protested. "I am a governess, but I am not penniless by any stretch of the imagination. My father is a gentleman, despite the circumstances of my birth, and he has been very generous with me."

"Pish posh!" Sissy waved her hand, defaulting to her usual manner when she heard something she did not like. "It's only money. I can hardly take it to my grave with me, can I? I might as well spend it on you. I'll only leave it to Barrett, otherwise, once I shuffle off the mortal coils. And he has enough funds already."

"Be that as it may—"

"No," Sissy answered firmly. "If you are permitted to pay for your own things, then you will choose your own things and that will see you in more drab, hideous colors. You are indulging an old woman, Minerva. I never had a daughter. I never had the opportunity to take one shopping for her debut or to purchase a trousseau. In short, allowing me to do these things for you will be to ease my old mind and soothe my poor wounded heart."

Minerva might have fallen for it had she not seen the calculating gleam in Sissy's eyes. "Now you're having me on."

Sissy's eyebrows shot up, almost to her silvered hairline. "Is it working?"

"Perhaps."

"Then it doesn't matter, does it?"

Minerva was halted from saying more by the appearance of the aforementioned dressmaker. The drawing room doors were flung open and the tiny, birdlike woman entered all but vibrating with energy. Like a hummingbird, she flitted in, kissing Sissy's cheeks and speaking in an accent that was positively most decidedly not French.

Bustling in after the dressmaker were easily half a dozen assistants carting in armloads full of parcels and bolts of fabric. It was an obscene amount. It was the sort of gross abundance she'd witnessed in homes when a girl was being prepared for her first Season.

"This is all too much," Minerva protested.

As if her words had summoned a pint-sized demon, the

dressmaker whirled on her. "It is not too much. I say if it is too much. And this, this is just enough! We will turn you from the cow's ear to the silk purse, no?"

"I believe you mean sow, as in pig. And that is hardly how I would categorize myself," Minerva protested, feeling more than moderately offended by the comparison.

The dressmaker reached out two fingers to touch the sleeve of Minerva's gown, almost as if it were something distasteful she'd been asked to dispose of. "I will determine that, Mademoiselle. And this travesty you wear... it must go. Burn it. Burn it now. It is not fit for rags."

Minerva felt the gathering storm of her temper, but then a small hand tugged at hers. She looked down into Meredith's upturned face.

"I want to see you in pretty gowns, Miss Stone. It'll be all right here. You can put on the drab ones when we're under the same roof as Peter again." The entire room went silent then, Meredith's innocent statement telling a truth universally understood by all women.

The dressmaker dropped her hand away from Minerva's sleeve, but her voice was much less biting when she said, "We will not burn it. We all must have our armor, no?"

Both embarrassed and strangely grateful, Minerva simply gave a curt nod. Then the true torment began. For the next hour, she was measured, poked, prodded, draped with one bolt of cloth after another until at last Sissy and the dressmaker, whose name she had discovered was simply Madame Jacqueline, were satisfied. All the while, three young women had been busily altering a trio of gowns that had been provided in some state of readiness.

"This one," Madame Jacqueline said, walking over to the busy seamstresses and lifting up the flowing skirts of one gown that was a strange shade somewhere between a slate blue and a dark violet. It altered with the changing light. "This one will be perfect on you."

"Excellent. You shall wear it for dinner," Sissy said. "I've just sent round a note to Barrett. He will be joining us."

"The duke?" Minerva asked nervously. Suddenly, she desperately longed for the invisibility that her current drab wardrobe provided. Being in his presence made her feel so terribly exposed.

"How many Barretts do you know?" Sissy asked with a laugh. "Of course, the duke. I cannot wait for him to see you—us. To see us. How surprised and happy he will be that we have elected to join him in the city. Naturally, he will come here to stay with us and not be bothered with that terribly common hotel."

Minerva let out a heavy sigh. Somehow, she would need to bring a halt to Sissy's not even thinly veiled attempts at matchmaking. There was no future for her and the Duke of Hargrieve—or if there was, it would certainly be an ignoble one for her. Dukes did not marry bastard governesses.

Except for Willa. And Lily. And Callie and Sophie.

The traitorous and slightly covetous voice inside her mind was one she could not afford to listen to. Her friends deserved their good fortune and their happy endings. And while she was not undeserving of such things, she wasn't foolish enough to expect them. It would only lead to disappointment.

Chapter Nine

I T WAS EVENING by the time he'd managed to have a bath, a meal and then a modicum of rest. After dressing, he'd headed downstairs. The missive had arrived just as Barrett had been leaving the hotel. The note remained shoved in his coat pocket as he toured the London house. With each successive room, his frown deepened.

It wasn't the extent of the damage which prompted his black mood. It was the lack. The fire had been limited to one room only—a bedroom upstairs that, if he were assessing the situation correctly, had been unused prior to the family's hasty decampment to his estate. While he had no doubt that the smoke would have been terrifying, he could not see why the family would have been forced to vacate. An airing of the house would have made it habitable.

The single charred room needed a new carpet, new drapes and wallpaper, some paint, and the furniture could certainly use with a good cleaning, but beyond that, it was hardly the catastrophe that Charlotte had claimed. He couldn't imagine that she would have gone to such lengths just to divest herself of her children. Had that been the case, she'd have simply plopped them in a carriage and sent them off to him to find appropriate boarding schools for the lot. No, she'd brought them there at such a time that she'd known he'd have to keep them under his roof for at least a short while. To what end?

If there was one thing he understood about Charlotte, there was always a plot or a scheme at the root of everything she did. He'd never known anyone more diabolically self-serving than his aunt.

Muttering a curse under his breath, Barrett turned and left the fire-damaged room and made his way down the corridor to what he thought was Charlotte's chamber. As he opened the door, he noticed one thing immediately. The bed was rumpled—as if someone had fled it hastily. And in the air, there was the scent of Charlotte's perfume. She hadn't gone to Bath, after all.

"Charlotte?" he shouted.

There was no immediate response. Of course, he hadn't anticipated that there would be. She might have even fled the house. He couldn't be sure. But whether she had or had not, what he said would be reported to her by the servants. He might pay them, but they'd learned over the years what happened to people who were not loyal to her.

Leaving her bedchamber, he found the butler waiting in the main corridor at the top of the stairs. He was the only servant who had remained when all others had been dismissed. Likely, Barrett thought, because he was very old and had nowhere else to go. "Where is she?"

"She, your grace?"

"Charlotte. Mrs. Entwhistle-Graves. Your mistress. My aunt. The bane of my existence," Barrett clarified.

"I could not say, your grace."

"Could not or will not?"

"Mrs. Entwhistle-Graves is not in the house, your grace. Are you quite well? Should I call a physician?" the butler answered.

Narrowing his eyes, Barrett glowered at the man. "I'm not a child to be bullied by you now. I'm also the person who, contrary to what Charlotte would have you believe, pays your wages. You will tell my aunt, upon her return, that I will find out what it is she's about and I will put a stop to it."

"If I should see her, your grace, I shall certainly inform her of your visit and your message."

"You do that," Barrett snapped and then pushed past the aging retainer to reach the stairs. He could still recall that same man holding him down as manacles had been placed on his wrists and he'd been dragged to a waiting cart to be carried off to Bedlam. The resentment ran deeper than he'd realized.

Once he exited the house, the tension that always plagued him whenever he entered those four walls faded. He despised that house and all the terrible memories it held for him.

Hailing a hack, he climbed onto the seat. It was the same driver who'd brought him there.

"Back to the 'otel with you, guv?"

Barrett reached into his pocket for a coin and found the note instead. Breaking the seal, he read it and cursed. "God save me from scheming women," he murmured.

"What was that? Where you 'eaded?" the driver asked.

"Bruton Street," Barrett answered. He'd need to figure out what Sissy had gotten into her head. Why the devil could no one in his family stay where he put them?

MINERVA WAS WEARING the gown Sissy and Madame Jacqueline had insisted upon. She couldn't deny that it was lovely, that the strangely hued fabric which seemed to shift from blue to purple with each flicker of the candles that lit the room made her feel beautiful. But even feeling beautiful, she did not feel entirely herself. It was as if she'd donned a costume when everyone else was wearing their normal attire.

The ratafia that she sipped was overly sweet, the taste of it lingering heavily on her tongue even as she simply toyed with the small glass it had been served in. Her gaze continued to drift toward the door, waiting for the duke to come thundering in, furious that his edicts regarding her and Meredith had been countermanded.

Sissy eyed her with disappointment. "Do not be so maudlin, Minerva! What can he say? The boy left the two of you in my care and I chose to bring you to London rather than rusticate in the countryside. What in heaven's name could be wrong with that?"

"I'm certain that was not his intent when he brought us to you, Aunt Sissy," Minerva replied. "I think the duke is a man who likes to be obeyed to the spirit of the law he has laid down rather than the letter of it. No, he did not forbid it, but that does not mean it will be a welcome surprise to find us here."

Sissy's lips pursed.

In anticipation, Minerva said, "Do not say it. If I never hear you say 'pish posh' again it will be too soon. I could be sacked for this. I could be sent packing right back to the Darrow School."

"Would that be so terrible? You cannot tell me you enjoy working for Charlotte!" Sissy insisted.

"No, I do not. But then Meredith would be alone. She's not at all like her siblings and could not be more different from her mother," Minerva answered. "I fear what will become of her in their midst if she does not have someone to shelter her."

It was Sissy's turn to heave a long-suffering sigh. "Very well. If Barrett is displeased, I shall take all the blame... and then we shall all retreat, posthaste, to Rossington Manor. Will that suffice, Miss Stone?"

"I shouldn't think that would be Miss Stone's decision."

The deep voice boomed from the doorway. He'd entered without allowing the butler to announce him. Turning to face the Duke of Hargrieve, Minerva knew what to expect. She knew that strange little stutter in her heartbeat would occur. She knew that the breath would rush from her lungs and her stomach would feel like swarms of butterflies were taking flight. But even being prepared for it did not lessen the intensity of those sensations. Nor did it do anything to prepare her for what he would look like—dressed in a dark frock coat, black brocade waistcoat and black trousers, the starched white linen of his shirt and cravat were a stark contrast. But above that, his chiseled, beard-shadowed jaw was hard and unyielding and his lips were firmed into a thin line that more than eloquently displayed his displeasure.

"Your grace," Minerva said nervously, getting to her feet.

"Relax, Miss Stone," he said, his tone easing somewhat from the cold snap it had been upon his entry. "I hold you blameless in this, but Sissy, that is another matter. Regardless, I have been summoned for dinner and dinner we shall have. When it is done, then my great-aunt and I shall have a reckoning after you have retired."

Minerva wanted to protest, but Sissy rose and placed a staying hand on her arm.

"Do not fret, my dear. My nephew is speaking metaphorically of reckonings. He would never actually harm me or anyone else, contrary to what others might whisper about him... and we all know that here, I think."

"Well, of course we do," Minerva agreed instantly.

"There, Barrett," Sissy said. "You have it. The one woman in all of England who immediately senses that you are inherently incapable of harming another. How remarkable."

"That's enough, Sissy."

Sissy smiled. "For now. Let us go in to dinner, shall we? I'm certain we've given the servants enough to gossip about."

Chapter Ten

TIME AND AGAIN, his gaze would find her. It was impossible not to do so. He'd thought her beautiful upon their first meeting. But dressed as she was, the brilliant color of her gown a perfect foil for her green eyes, and the neckline revealing just enough to make him yearn to see more—he was drowning in it, in his obsession with her. And that obsession was one he could ill afford. There were things at play that he did not understand. Charlotte's plots and schemes worried him. The young boy that was even now being tormented in Bedlam.

If nothing else, Sissy's appearance with Meredith and Miss Stone in tow would offer one solution. He could bring the boy there rather than wait for an assessment of the damage and cleaning to his own house. And he could only imagine that Miss Stone would be a soothing presence for the child.

No. Not the child. John.

If there was one thing that Barrett understood about Bedlam, it stripped one of dignity, of any sort of humanity, including one's name. Boy. Idiot. Imbecile. Murderer. He'd been called many things during his incarceration there. But no one had ever used his name. Whatever else he could do for him, Barrett would give him back at least that much.

"Sissy, I'll be retrieving Charlotte's son from the asylum tomorrow and bringing him here," he stated. "I'll need you to have a room ready for him. It can't be just a normal bedchamber. He will have no concept of such spaces. Something simple with only a bed and perhaps a washbasin in it. Anything more might be… overwhelming to him."

Sissy looked up at him then. "There is a small bedchamber off the schoolroom on the third floor that is unused. I can have it readied for him. It will leave him in close proximity to Minerva during the nights. That way if he has nightmares—"

"That isn't a question," Barrett stated. "He will have nightmares. Such a place always leaves its mark. Are you prepared for another charge, Miss Stone? One who may prove very challenging, indeed?"

Miss Stone placed her wine glass back on the table. She hadn't been drinking it so much as toying with it throughout dinner. But when she met his gaze, he could see something in her gaze that bothered him. Pity. Sissy had clearly been very free with information.

"I hope that I am. Until I meet him, until I know what sort of ailment prompted Mrs. Entwhistle-Graves to put him in such a place to begin with, I cannot say with certainty. And Meredith was so young, beyond his inability to speak, she cannot recall much. But I confess, why did she keep it a secret?"

Sissy sighed. "My dear, most families of quality would hide such a thing. To have a child committed to an asylum—well, we all know how society treats those whom they feel are tainted with madness, don't we?"

Miss Stone shook her head. "Well, no. I understand that part of it. But with you being unmarried, when Mrs. Entwhistle-Graves gave birth to a son, who for all intents and purposes appeared to be perfectly healthy at the time—I assume—was your heir. She had given birth to the heir of the dukedom. I can't imagine that she would not have crowed victoriously about such a thing. Does it not strike you as odd?"

Barrett had not considered that. In truth, from the moment he had learned of the boy's existence and where he was currently being held, that had been all he could think of—to get him out. But there was an undeniable truth in Miss Stone's assessment. Charlotte would have loved nothing better than to boast about her child one day ascending to the role of duke. She'd have droned on endlessly about how she would not be kept to such miserly standards when her child was in charge of the estates. And she would have taken every opportunity to remind him of his own ineligibility and the likelihood that he would ever find a woman who would be willing to overlook his storied past, regardless of whether or not she thought him guilty.

"Perhaps there was some indication even at birth that the child had some sort of disability," Sissy suggested. "Otherwise, you are quite right. Charlotte would have gloated terribly over such a thing. She'd have given poor Barrett no peace at all."

"Whatever her reasons," Barrett stated, "I intend to ferret it all out. I've tolerated her wickedness and her many schemes for long enough. I will be certain that Meredith and John are well cared for. I will do what I can for Peter and Willis, within reason and assuming they can behave with some degree of honor and morality. But I will not be supporting Charlotte anymore. She will have to find her own way in the world after this."

Dinner continued in the same vein. They talked of less serious topics, Sissy clearly doing her best to play matchmaker. It was quite obvious that she'd taken Miss Stone under her wing in the hopes of facilitating a match between them. If only she knew what his feelings for the lovely Miss Stone were! He could not afford to reveal himself to either of them.

Miss Stone was not for him. She was too kind, too pure, too good. For all that he did not believe he was guilty of the crimes others attributed to him, any woman he married would be tainted by his reputation. He could not do that to her. It would be the worst sort of selfishness.

When the meal ended, they retreated to the drawing room once more. There was a pianoforte in one corner of the room. Without being asked, Miss Stone simply walked toward the instrument and seated herself there. Without any sheet music, she began to play, her fingers flying nimbly over the keys. The sweet melody she played was a reprieve from having to make polite conversation. So he settled himself into a chair by the fireplace and simply watched her.

Her expression seemed to shift and change with each note. It was, perhaps, the first time he had seen her truly unguarded, when she hadn't been trying to project an image of self-reliance and independence, when there was no false bravado in the face of the very real threat Peter had posed to her. In that moment, as she gave herself over to the music that seemed to flow from her as much as from the instrument she played, she appeared to be totally free. He envied her that. The closest he had ever come to that feeling was riding out over the fields, the horse thundering beneath him at full speed and the wind tearing at his hair. But even then, he couldn't escape what was inside him. *The uncertainty.*

Not recalling murdering his entire family did not mean that he had not done it. Believing he was innocent was not the same as knowing he was innocent and, until he could know that fully, Miss Stone would do well to remain guarded and aloof.

Chapter Eleven

MINERVA TOSSED AND turned in her bed, unable to sleep. Meredith had come to her room and climbed into bed with her. That had become an almost nightly occurrence since the child's mother had left. But there was no comfort to be had in sharing a bed with a child. It seemed the smaller the person, the more space they required. As she removed Meredith's elbow from her ribs for the umpteenth time, she sighed into the darkness.

The little girl made a sound of protest as Minerva once more disturbed her. Feeling guilty for that, especially as she had been through so much of late and clearly needed rest, Minerva rose from the bed quietly and slipped on her wrapper. Easing from the room, she closed the door with a soft snick and made her way along the corridor. Perhaps she'd find a book in the library to help settle her mind.

From the moment Mrs. Entwhistle-Graves had employed her, Minerva had not liked the woman. But not liking her did not necessarily mean thinking her a villain. Now, as more information came to light, she could only think that perhaps the woman had locked her child away for some nefarious purpose. It weighed heavily on her mind. But that wasn't keeping her awake. Her insomnia could be laid squarely at the feet of his grace, the Duke of Hargrieve.

Aunt Sissy was still matchmaking. Whether she wished to admit it or not, and whether or not they were willing to be matched, the woman was relentless. Of course, Minerva had to admit that what Meredith had told the elderly woman was true. Whenever she and the duke were in the same room together, they were constantly sneaking glances at one another. She could not stop thinking of that moment just outside the gallery, when she'd nearly fallen after Peter had released her and the duke had caught her against him to steady her. The memory of his arms closing about her, of the hard wall of his chest as it had pressed against her—they were permanently emblazoned in her mind.

For a woman who prided herself on being sensible and pragmatic, her ridiculous infatuation with him was unbearable. He was a duke. And dukes did not marry governesses, as a rule. They specifically did not marry illegitimate governesses.

But they did take them as mistresses.

That traitorous thought had been circulating in her mind for the better part of the journey to London. A half-formed thought at first, it had begun to take shape fully over the course of the day.

It was not a possibility that any respectable young woman would entertain. But then, she was not respectable. It was the path her own mother had chosen, after all. By all, quite happily if memory served her correctly. Until her mother had passed away from a fever when she was just a bit older than Meredith was now, they'd lived quite happily in the small house her father had provided for them. He'd visited them often, spoiling them both with trinkets and gifts. But it had been the attention he lavished on them that had been truly magical. She had no doubt that he'd loved her mother and that her mother had loved him. Whatever the more practical elements of their arrangement, the feelings had been quite genuine. Could she do that? Could she give herself to a man in that way, knowing that she would never have all of him?

It was presumptuous of her to think that the duke would even consider her for such an arrangement. For all she knew, he might already have a mistress tucked away somewhere that he was perfectly content with. But if so, why did she occasionally catch glances from him that seemed to be filled with such longing? Or was she simply projecting her own desires onto him? Was it better to have a few stolen moments of happiness—of passion and joy—than to never to know it at all?

Taking the stairs very carefully in the dim light that filtered in from the windows, she made her way to the lower floor and the small library that was opposite the drawing room. Opening the door, she stepped inside and turned to close it softly behind her. When she turned back, she noted the lamp still burning on one of the tables. Her gaze snapped around the room until she caught sight of her fellow restless guest. It was the duke himself, standing near the fireplace with a glass of brandy in one hand and a book in the other.

"I'm sorry," she murmured softly. "I didn't realize—it was not my intent to disturb you."

"It is most certainly too late for that," he said. "But don't let it stop you. What are you doing roaming the halls so late, Miss Stone?"

"I couldn't sleep," she confessed. "I thought perhaps I'd find something very dull to read to combat the issue."

He smirked and raised the book he held. "*Thornton's Treatise on Farming Innovations*. I can attest to its dullness. Let us hope it proves more successful as a sedative for you than it has for me."

With her heart pounding in her chest beating a wild tattoo, she stepped forward and closed the distance between them. As he passed the book to her, their fingers brushed and she could feel the heat of his skin against hers. "Thank you. I'm certain it will work," she replied. Because the moment was so charged, so potent, she attempted a forced laugh and added, "I've no interest in farming at all."

"What does interest you, Miss Stone? Other than music. Clearly what you have is beyond a simple affinity for it. It's a gift... truly," he said.

Minerva blushed. "My mother played. Beautifully. I am a

novice in comparison. When I play, I feel close to her, as if I'm sharing that with her."

"How old were you when you lost your mother?"

Minerva sighed. "Not old enough. I was nine years old. But I think one is never old enough to say goodbye to their parent. I am lucky that I still have my father, though we do not see one another as often as we once did."

"By his choice... or by yours?"

"Neither, I suppose. He is a kind man but one who lives a rather dissolute lifestyle that it would not behoove me to be seen entering or leaving his home regardless of our relationship. There are other people, other men, who frequent his house that would... well, I daresay that they are simply older versions of Peter," she finished lamely.

"Ah, I see."

"When I was still at the Darrow School, he would come there," she said. Idly, her hands wandered over the cover of the book, tracing the intricate designs on the binding. Anything to keep them steady and away from the man in front of her. "We would have tea and he would bring gifts. But it wasn't the same as when my mother was alive. I think he has never recovered from her death. And his wife lives separately from him in the country for most of the year. They were never happy together. She would certainly never permit me to visit him there."

"You miss him." It wasn't a question but an observation.

Minerva's lips queried upwards, her smile no doubt reflecting her bittersweet feelings. "I miss him as he was then. I think my father's grief over my mother, coupled with his dissatisfaction with life in general, has made him bitter. He is not the same man now that he was when I was a child. Do you miss your father? After so long?"

He cocked his head to one side, considering the question. "Not always. I've lived more of my life without him now than I did with him. But there are moments when I desperately want his advice—the benefit of his wisdom. I miss my brothers, however. I miss them more often because I never anticipated that I would not have them in my life. My father was older, so it was always understood that I would be without him one day."

"You truly do not remember what happened the day they died?" she asked.

His expression did not go cold, as much as it went blank. And then the silence stretched between them until it became unbearable.

"That was a terribly impertinent question," Minerva offered "I am sorry. It is none of my business. I should not have asked."

"It isn't impertinent. I understand that is difficult for people to grasp that I have some recollection of such a tragic event," he replied haltingly. "It isn't just that I witnessed their murders and the trauma of it that robbed me of my memory. I was struck on the head with what is believed to have been the butt of a gun. I was completely insensible when I wandered to a nearby farmer's house. I could barely speak at all. None of it was coherent."

Minerva blinked. She'd certainly never heard that. The rumors had always alluded to the fact that he had escaped unharmed. That had been the primary source of everyone's suspicions. Why had the murderers spared him... unless he was the murderer? "I didn't know. I'm so sorry. And then your aunt—"

"Charlotte knew. Charlotte knew all the details. In fact, it was those very details which allowed her to have me locked away in Bedlam just as she has her youngest son. To what end, I still do not understand. But if there is one thing I know about Charlotte, it's that there is always some avenue of personal gain in everything she does. Greedy. Avaricious. Unconscionable. Meredith is better off for her having left, as cold as that may sound. It is only a pity she didn't abandon her elder sons earlier. They might have become better men for it."

She could not disagree with that assessment. She also could not afford to continue the conversation. Continuing to stand there in the dark, talking to him in only her nightrail and wrapper while the rest of the house was abed—that was an exercise in foolishness.

"I should go," she said. "Thank you for the book. I'm certain it will help."

Before she could turn to walk away, his hand shot out, encircling her wrist. It was a gentle grasp, one she could have easily broken free from if she chose. But she had no wish to break that contact. Even that simple touch was like the jolts created by the electrifying machines she'd seen on display.

"Miss Stone... I know what Sissy is about. I see where her fantastical imaginings are leading her and I do not wish you to be disappointed."

And just like that, the spark she'd felt withered and died. In its place, she felt only humiliation. "I understand perfectly, your grace. I would never have imagined that a man of your elevated standing would entertain any notions of romance or marriage for a girl like me."

"A girl like you? What precisely does that mean?"

"A bastard, your grace. A governess. A servant." The last escaped with more bitterness than she'd intended. "I know what I am. And I know that I will never be the sort of woman a peer, much less a duke, would marry."

≫≫≪≪

HE'D INSULTED HER. Unintentionally, of course. More than that, he'd hurt her. Her pride certainly, rather than her heart, but such a wound pricked all the same. "Miss Stone... Minerva..."

It was a mistake to use her given name, to foster the intimacy between them that had already become unbearable. "You mistake my meaning. The fault, if such a term can be used, does not lie with you. No woman who marries me will ever know a moment's peace. There will be no invitations to parties and balls. There will only be gossip and misery—pointing fingers and indelicate whispers as everyone calls her the wife of a murderer."

"Clearly, I am overwhelmed with invitations to parties and balls as it is, your grace. Why on earth would such things matter to me when they are obviously never going to be a part of my life anyway?" she snapped. "Please let go of my arm."

"I only meant that—any woman who marries me will not have the same sort of life that she would marrying another peer. And you deserve that sort of life, Minerva. You deserve a man who can give you better than what you currently have."

She blinked at him, her shock quite evident even in the dimness of the room. "What I deserve? What about you? What do you deserve? Have you given that any thought at all?"

"Until I can say without even a whisper of doubt that I am not guilty of what others accuse of me, I do not know what I deserve." The admission cost him. It was something he'd thought frequently but never uttered aloud. To hear those words, to hear the doubt in his own voice, echoing back to him, was a reality that he was not prepared for. Without thinking, he let her go, dropping her wrist and turning away from her so suddenly that she let out a gasp, almost as if she feared him. That only underscored his feelings of unworthiness. He had no right to want her. And every moment in her presence was a dangerous temptation.

It was the warmth of her small hand on his shoulder, a gentle touch that soothed and inflamed him all at once, that had him turning, glancing back at her.

"You may have doubts about your innocence, but I do not. You could never have done what they say... I knew that even before I knew of your injury. It would be impossible. If you wish to put barriers between us, let them be honest ones."

It was the unwavering faith he'd heard in her voice that robbed him of his last defense. She had no doubt of his innocence and that belief unlocked something with him. It freed him in a way nothing else ever had. Without thought, he whirled and pulled her into his arms, holding her so tightly against him that she had to tilt her head back to meet his gaze. He scanned her face, looking for some sign of fear, some sign of protest. All he saw was her lips parted in surprise, a sweet and tempting invitation.

"Tell me to let you go," he demanded hoarsely. "Tell me not to kiss you until we are both mad with it. Tell me!"

She gazed back at him for the longest moment, her eyes sparkling with reflected candlelight. "If only I could... because, God help me, I do not want you to let me go. And if you do not kiss me, I may go mad from the lack."

"Then God help us both," he muttered. And with the last vestiges of his willpower slipping away, he lowered his head and pressed his lips to hers, tasting the sweetness that had tormented his dreams from the moment he'd first laid eyes on her.

Chapter Twelve

S HE HAD NEVER been kissed before. Certainly, she was not
unfamiliar with the particulars. Many times, she'd witnessed
passionate embraces between her parents when she was supposed
to have been abed. There had been countless whispered
conversations amongst the girls at school, all of them followed by
giggles and squeals and even a few sounds of disgust. As she'd
gotten older, there had been scandalous and slightly salacious
novels with dark, brooding heroes who'd swept the innocent
heroine into his arms and introduced her to a world of florid yet
vaguely depicted passion.

Nothing in her life could have prepared her for the feeling of
being so close to him, of being trapped in an embrace she had no
wish to escape from. In fact, she would have gladly let it go on
forever. Because unlike the other times in her life when a
member of the opposite sex had wrapped his arms about her, she
felt safe. Cherished. Protected. Sheltered. Desired. He didn't hold
her tightly to prevent her escape. Had she protested, he would
have let her go immediately.

When his lips finally touched hers, when she could taste the
hint of brandy that he'd consumed and something else that was
simply him, she let out a sigh of contentment. It was as if she'd
found something lost, something she treasured. That touch
brought both relief and frustration—relief because it had

happened and frustration because, as glorious as it was, it was not enough.

As his lips moved over hers, mapping every curve and contour, his hands roamed her back, traveled the span of her waist and then settled low on her hips, holding her to him intimately. Not even a breath separated their bodies and she could feel the hard planes and ridges of his body against her, noting the differences between them with both curiosity and appreciation.

When he nipped her lower lip ever so gently, she gasped in surprise and pleasure at that unexpected sensation. That had apparently been his intent. His tongue swept boldly in, sliding sensuously against her own in a way that sent a rush of heat through her. She could feel her pulse pounding furiously and warmth pooling low in her belly. Where her breasts were crushed against his chest, her skin tingled and she could feel her nipples hardening into taut peaks. It might only have been a kiss, and yet she felt it to her toes. Not a part of her was unaffected by the sensual onslaught.

It might have been minutes or hours. Time stood still. The entire world faded from her consciousness. Only he existed there with her—just the two of them and the hot, drugging sensation of his mouth on hers. And then the kiss broke, his lips parting from hers as she whimpered in protest at the loss. That whimper quickly transformed into one of pleasure as he began to kiss a path along her jawline, her neck, and lower to her collarbone just visible above the edge of her wrapper. When he dipped his tongue into the hollow at the base of her throat, licking her skin, she felt as if she were on fire. She wanted nothing more than to shake off the heavy, quilted wrapper and feel the cool night air on her heated flesh.

Somewhere in the house, glass shattered. It was loud and violent—no mere glass or vase being knocked from a table, but something far more sinister. He pulled back instantly and put her behind him, standing between her and whatever threat they might encounter.

"What happened?" Minerva whispered, still dazed and shaken from the kiss.

"It sounded like a window," he said. "Housebreakers or... perhaps something worse."

"What could be worse?" she asked.

He frowned. "I had a number of accidents and delays on the way to London, Minerva. And the more time I've had to reflect on the matter, the less likely it seems that they were a coincidence. More, it seems like someone was making every effort to see my arrival here delayed or, perhaps, something worse. Also, Charlotte lied about the house."

"There was a fire," she insisted. "When we were awakened, the corridors were filled with smoke."

"Oh, I've no doubt of it. But the damage is minimal. A good airing and the house would be habitable," he said. "She need not have traveled all the way to Yorkshire and left her children in my care. Also, I have good reason to think she is not in Bath at all, but here in London."

Minerva's eyes widened. "You think she is behind it all, don't you?"

"I do," he stated. "And you gave me the motive. If I die, Charlotte's secret child is my heir. But if she's had him labeled as insane or deficient in some way, then Willis, who is only a month from reaching his majority, will be his guardian and will have control of the estate."

It was diabolical, but not out of the question. In fact, it explained so much about her employer's behavior. "Let's go investigate the breaking glass and see what we have."

"Absolutely not. I will go investigate and you will remain here, well hidden. If it's someone Charlotte has hired to do away with me, I will not risk putting you in danger."

"But—"

"No buts," he said, removing her hand from his arm. "Wait here. Do not leave this room. If you are discovered in my company, you would be ruined, Minerva. I would not do that to you. Please?"

A terrible thought occurred to her then. He wasn't protecting her reputation so much as he was protecting his own freedom. If they were caught in a compromising position together, he was honorable enough that he would not leave her to suffer the scandal. But avoiding the scandal altogether would save him from having to make an offer for her.

Gathering the last shreds of her wounded pride about her, Minerva nodded. "Fine. I shall wait here for a suitable length of time. Then I will return to my room. What happened between us tonight... it will not happen again. It was a mistake and should not be compounded further."

He searched her face for a moment, clearly puzzled by her response. Then he nodded. "Of course. As you wish. Five minutes, at least. If you encounter any servants investigating the sound, tell them it was the breaking glass that awakened you and you went to look for the source."

Her smile was somewhat bitter as she commented, "You are rather shockingly adept at subterfuge. Goodnight, your grace."

BARRETT WAS PUZZLED by her reaction, by the immediate reversal of her behavior from wildly passionate to coldly rebuffing him. But there was no time to solve that mystery at the moment. There were more immediate pressing matters.

Taking another lamp from the desk and lighting it, he left her there as he emerged into the corridor and crossed into the drawing room, the only other room on the main floor to face the street. It was not difficult to discern the source of the noise. Curtains from the window on the farthest side of the room were fluttering in the breeze. But it did not appear anyone had entered the house. Instead, they'd thrown a brick through those windows. It lay on the ornate rug before the settee, a note crudely tied around it.

Crossing to the projectile, he stooped to pick it up. When he freed the note, he found only a single word scrawled on the damp paper. *Murderer.*

There was no question that the note was intended for him. But who had thrown it through that particular window? Who had followed him from Mivart's to the Mayfair house and from there to a house that he had no connection to beyond his aunt being a friend of the home's owner. Someone was watching him closely. Why?

What would have happened if that brick had been tossed into the library instead? What if it had struck a lamp or candelabra and set the entire house ablaze? Recalling Minerva's—no, Miss Stone's—assertion that what had happened between them was a mistake and could not be repeated, he found himself in agreement, though for very different reasons.

He was a target of someone for reasons he could not fully understand. But being close to her would put her in danger and that was not something that he could live with. They would return to Griffingate as soon as possible. To do less would be foolish. In his home, he could protect them. In his home, they were not surrounded by potential suspects at every turn. The crowded London streets were a perfect place for a villain to simply disappear. On his isolated estate, anyone who meant them harm could be easily exposed.

He'd just reached his decision when the sleepy-eyed butler entered. Tucking the note into his pocket, he passed the brick to the befuddled retainer. "Vandals," he explained. "Or drunkards, perhaps, given the hour."

"Perhaps, your grace," the butler agreed, though he was clearly suspicious.

"Have the window boarded up for the night, and we will see about commissioning a replacement tomorrow. In the meantime, I must go out. I will look around and see if I can find any sign of the culprit."

"Yes, your grace."

Exiting the drawing room, he could just see the swish of Miss Stone's wrapper as she made her way up the stairs. He followed her with his gaze, willing her to look back against his own better judgment. She paused at the top, her hand on the rail. But she did not look back at him. After a moment's hesitation, she turned and disappeared down the upper corridor.

Cursing himself and her, Barrett left the house and made his way two streets over to the darkened home of Lord Highcliff. The man was not sleeping, no matter how dark the house was. If there was one thing he knew about Highcliff, it was that the man never slept.

Chapter Thirteen

"W HAT DO YOU mean he isn't here?" Barrett demanded of the dressing gown-clad butler.

"Lord Highcliff has not returned home for some time, your grace," the butler replied. "And I am not at liberty to disclose his location. It would be indiscreet."

Barrett wanted to throttle the man. It wasn't his fault, of course. And, in truth, his foul temper had far more to do with the way he'd parted company with Minerva—Miss Stone—than Lord Highcliff's absence. The truth, quite simply, was that Highcliff was a very difficult man to track down on purpose. Barrett couldn't say precisely what role it was that Highcliff fulfilled for the crown but there was little doubt that it was a far cry from the dandy he played while out and about in society.

"Do you know when he will return?" Barrett asked.

"No, your grace. I do not. If you wish to leave a message for him, I will happily deliver it when he returns," the butler stated, as if it were a normal call and not some sort of urgent situation that necessitated someone knocking on the door in the wee hours of the morning.

"No. That's fine. I can't imagine that I will remain in London long enough for that to matter," Barrett said. "I will write to Highcliff about the situation later. It needs to be explained more thoroughly than a simple note would manage. It will take a treatise."

The butler simply stood there, impassive. He said nothing further as he was clearly waiting for Barrett to make some statement of departure.

"Thank you. Good evening," Barrett finally muttered and turned to walk away. He was irritated more with himself than with Highcliff. The man, contrary to what many believed of him, did have responsibilities, after all.

Heading across Park Lane toward the house Sissy was occupying on Mount Street, he was cursing his luck just as he cursed Miss Stone and the temptation she provided. Kissing her had been a mistake. There was no doubt of that. But it irked him beyond measure that she was the one to have said so first. It wounded his already fragile pride. For her to have such immediate regrets made him question if perhaps he had overplayed his hand, if he'd frightened her or taken greater liberties than she'd intended to permit. In the moment, it certainly hadn't seemed so, but it would be foolish not to consider the possibility. After all, he'd been quite distracted with his own enjoyment of that brief but electrifying moment.

Distracted as he was by thoughts of Miss Stone, it took a moment or two for him to become aware enough of his surroundings to recognize that something was terribly wrong. There was an echoing set of footfalls. Someone was following him and was incredibly careful to keep their footsteps perfectly synchronized. Had it not been for him stepping to one side to avoid a small puddle, he might never have realized it.

Cautious now, with the skin prickling at the back of his neck and his hair standing on end, he measured each step. He scanned each shadowy doorway or entrance to darkened mews. And when they pounced, he was ready.

There were two altogether—one following him and one lying in wait just ahead. Both had cloths tied over their faces and wore hats to disguise their identities. Which meant they were known to him in some way, or such an effort would not have been necessary.

As the first one raised his pistol, it was clear they expected him to be an easy target. But he'd come prepared. Tucked into his coat was a short sword which he had learned, during his time at the school Highcliff had arranged for him to attend, to wield with deadly efficiency. The first one was dispatched quickly enough. One wicked slash to the man's forearm and he could no longer wield the pistol he'd brandished, dropping it to the paving stones with a clatter as he clutched the profusely bleeding wound.

The other attacker proved to be a bit more skilled and far more difficult to disarm. He carried a blade with a longer reach. He did not have the same degree of proficiency but his weapon of choice helped to make up some of the advantage. Every thrust was countered, every advance blocked. And minutes later, with the other attacker disarmed, both fled into the darkness, disappearing into the depths of the mews.

Barrett started to go after them, but then reconsidered. They could already be hiding, lying in wait again. And they would have the advantage in such close quarters. He could be overpowered by both of them when he had no room to maneuver out of their grasps. Reluctantly, he returned his sword to its sheath and continued toward his temporary abode. It would be dawn soon, and the last thing he needed was for someone to see him on the street in the wee hours with a sword on his person. The gossip mill would be whirring by tea time.

SLEEP HAD BEEN as elusive after her trip to the library as it had been before it. The reasons had been entirely different, of course. Following her encounter in the library with the duke—a lapse in judgment that had prompted deep feelings of shame—her earlier questions had been answered. Whatever path her mother had chosen, it was clear to Minerva that she was not the sort of woman who could ever be a man's mistress. It would rob her of her soul one small piece at a time until she had nothing left. However much he stirred her blood, however much he made her heart race and her skin heat with desire, she could not be that woman. And he would never ask her to be anything else.

Getting up from the chaise where she'd spent the remainder of the night, Minerva crossed to the washstand and splashed water onto her face in an effort to clear her mind of the whirling, negative thoughts that plagued her. When the effort failed, she removed the heavy plait that contained her hair and brushed the blonde strands into some semblance of order before pinning them up into a smooth coil.

She might not feel respectable, but she could still look it.

Moving behind the screen that had been placed near the fire for dressing, she changed from her nightclothes into a simple day dress. The sun would be up soon. The Darrow School would be abuzz with activity from daybreak on. Effie was an early riser and always had been. Minerva felt desperately in need of the other woman's calming presence. She needed guidance, not on what to do, but on what she had become. Effie had been her role model, her aspiration. And Effie would never have been caught kissing a forbidden man in a library in the wee hours of the morning. *Not even Lord Highcliff.*

Dressed for the day, she emerged from behind the screen to find Meredith sitting up in bed. The small girl stared at her suspiciously.

"Are you leaving like Mother did?"

Minerva shook her head. "No. I will not leave you, Meredith. I had thought I might go visit the Darrow School today and have a word with Miss Euphemia Darrow, the headmistress there and my mentor. Would you like to accompany me?"

"Will we be leaving before or after breakfast?" the little girl asked.

"Before... I thought we might go and have breakfast at the Darrow School. It might be nice for you to meet some other girls close to your age."

Meredith nodded. "I'd like that. I've never been around other children... well, besides Peter. Willis was always so much older that he was never much like a child. And poor John—I can barely recall him."

That would certainly explain why Meredith rarely sounded like a child, Minerva thought sadly. Her mother had kept her so isolated and so surrounded by adults that she'd never really had an opportunity to be a little girl. "Meredith, have you ever played?"

"Pianoforte? Of course. You've been teaching me," the child replied.

"No, Meredith. Played with dolls, or climbed trees, or skipped rope, or played knucklebones?" Minerva clarified.

"I had a doll once but Peter broke it. And Mother said I was careless to leave it where he might find it," Meredith answered. "But I think I would like to have one—with pretty golden hair like yours. Do you think Cousin Barrett would get one for me?"

"Oh, I'm quite certain he will," Minerva stated. "But I think I may have one you will like. I've had it since I was a girl, but she's very pretty. She's in a trunk, tucked away at the Darrow School. We will fetch her when we go there today."

With that, Meredith was up and out of bed, rushing to the washstand to see to her morning ablutions. Minerva waited patiently until the girl was done then helped her to plait her hair and create some semblance of order out of the wild curls. When Meredith was dressed, they walked together down the stairs but were stopped in their tracks in the foyer by the appearance of the duke. He'd just stepped in from outdoors.

Minerva took in his appearance in a glance. Dirty clothing, a split lip, blood on his sleeve from what appeared to be some sort of knife wound. There were dark hollows beneath his eyes that likely matched her own.

"Have you been stabbed, your grace?"

"Sliced, actually... a bit of a sword fight. Not at all what I expected when returning from Lord Highcliff's home," he answered levelly. "Where are you going?"

"Meredith and I are going to visit the Darrow School," Minerva stated. "I thought it might be good for her to meet some girls her own age... unless you have some objection, of course. I realize that, socially, the students there are not her equal."

"I have no objection to the Darrow School or any of its students, current or former," he replied. "But you cannot go alone. Not after the events of last evening. I will accompany you."

It was precisely the thing she had hoped to avoid... more time in his company. But taking in his battered appearance, the brick that had been thrown through the window the night before, and everything else they were currently facing, she knew she could not risk Meredith's safety for the sake of her own battered pride. "We will await you in the drawing room."

Chapter Fourteen

T HE CARRIAGE RIDE to the Darrow School was completed in utter silence. Even Meredith refrained from speaking. But precocious as she was, nothing escaped the child. Her gaze passed back and forth between the two of them and she was clearly quite aware of the tension that existed there.

Thankfully, it was a short distance and the normally busy streets of Mayfair were not yet congested with the ladies and gentlemen of the *ton* paying their calls and doing the necessary social dance to see and be seen. Upon their arrival, Barrett climbed down first. Meredith was next, allowing him to lift her out without protest and even granting him a rather charming giggle. But when he offered Minerva his hand, she refused it. Instead, she grasped the side of the carriage and stepped down on her own, eschewing any assistance at all.

He stayed back, not entirely sure of his welcome, as Minerva marched toward the door and lifted the heavy brass knocker. It fell against the plate, the strike resounding in the quiet morning air. After a moment, a rather harried-looking woman of indeterminate years with a plump figure and gray hair answered the door. Upon seeing Minerva, she immediately made a sound that conveyed great relief and no small amount of joy before engulfing the younger woman in a tight embrace.

"Oh, Miss Minerva! I'm so glad you've come home. You'll

talk some sense into her! She's fit to be tied right now... and it's all because of *him!*"

"Mrs. Wheaton, where is Effie?" Minerva asked softly.

"Upstairs. He's in her room," the woman said, clearly scandalized.

Minerva went completely still then, her shoulders drawn back in shock. "Is he ill?"

"Injured, Miss. Near dead he has been... more's the pity he didn't slide on into the great beyond if you ask me," the woman muttered. Then her gaze caught on Meredith. Immediately, her face flooded with warmth. She went from downcast and bitter to jovial in a second. "Well, who might you be? What a darling girl you are! Look at those curls. Tight as a spring, they are. Come in! Come in! Let me feed you something."

"His grace will be accompanying us, Mrs. Wheaton," Minerva informed the woman.

At that point, Mrs. Wheaton's gaze settled on him and it was like ice had been poured over him. The woman clearly did not have a high opinion of the opposite sex. But then the woman turned, disappearing into the house and ushering Meredith in with her. Closing the distance between himself and Minerva, he asked, "Who is this he she speaks of?"

"Lord Highcliff," Minerva replied. "He and Miss Darrow are of long acquaintance."

"I need to see him," Barrett insisted.

"Well, I suppose that will be up to Miss Darrow. If he is too severely hurt to have visitors then you will simply have to wait. Duke or no, Effie rules this house with a firm but fair hand," Minerva replied. Then she stepped over the threshold, leaving him to follow in her tracks or be left behind entirely. She'd made it perfectly clear that she did not care one way or the other.

Following behind her, he entered a bastion of female energy that left him immediately aware that he was well out of his depth.

MINERVA LEFT MEREDITH in Mrs. Wheaton's capable hands. The little girl was clearly charmed by the woman's effusive warmth and obvious adoration of all children. It was always Mrs. Wheaton who managed to turn the tide for even the most difficult and guarded of young girls who found their way to the Darrow School. The woman's background was a mystery, but her heart was certainly of the purest gold.

Climbing the stairs, she bypassed the private bedchambers that many of the older girls were given and the dormitory rooms that the younger girls all shared. She made her way along the corridor to the more luxuriously appointed, though not by much, room which Effie had maintained for herself. It was small by most standards. A double bed, washbasin and wardrobe filled it to the point of making it seem overcrowded. But each of those pieces of furniture was exquisite, as was the Persian carpet which bedecked the floor and the velvet drapes which covered the windows.

Knocking softly, Effie called out for her to enter. But when she opened the door, the room that greeted her was not the normally tidy boudoir of her mentor. It had been converted fully into a sick room. A chair had been placed beside the bed and Effie was seated in it, looking weary enough that she herself might need a sick bed before long.

In her bed, Lord Highcliff reclined against the pillows, his normally swarthy face ashen and pale. His black locks were dull and lank against his forehead and a heavy growth of beard covered his chin and jawline, a testament to how many days he had been there.

"Effie, you look terrible," Minerva stated without malice. It was a simple observation. "You have exhausted yourself caring for him and if you do not rest soon, you will be of no use to anyone. Not yourself and certainly not Lord Highcliff."

Effie looked at her, the blue shadows beneath her eyes making her appear far older than her years. "I'm afraid to leave him. If he awakens—he's had terrible nightmares, Minerva. Some are not just figments of his fevered mind, but terrible memories he would not wish others to know."

"And no one will know the difference between the two but you and Lord Highcliff himself," Minerva replied.

Effie blinked in surprise at that. "Oh. I hadn't—well, that had not crossed my mind."

"Of course, it hadn't. You've worn yourself ragged. Get up. Go to one of the few empty rooms in this monstrous house and go to bed. Sleep before you fall over," Minerva insisted. "If you need me to, I will sit with him in your stead."

It was Effie's turn to state the obvious. "You are not exactly refreshed yourself. I know why I had a sleepless night. Why did you?"

"Men are the plague of all women," Minerva answered. "But we can discuss it later."

"There are no men in Mrs. Entwhistle-Graves' house, unless you count her sons."

Minerva sighed. "I am no longer in Mrs. Entwhistle-Graves' house. She moved us all to the countryside to the estate of her nephew, the Duke of Hargrieve. Then she promptly abandoned us all. So, my situation has changed though my employment has not. Go rest, Effie. I mean it. You are pale, your eyes are shadowed and you have lost weight you could ill-afford to sacrifice. All for a man who only ever causes you pain."

"You sound like Mrs. Wheaton," Effie replied, though she did rise from her chair. In doing so, she nearly collapsed to the floor. She had to place one hand on the back of the chair and one hand on the nearby bedpost to steady herself.

"Men have some uses after all," Minerva mused. Walking to the door, she called out into the corridor until one of the younger girls came running. "There is a gentleman downstairs. Mrs. Wheaton will know where to find him. We require his assistance here."

"What are you doing?" Effie demanded after sinking back into the chair.

"It is quite obvious that you will not make it to another chamber under your own power. I may have my own issues with the duke, but he is gentleman enough not to let you fall on your face."

After a few moments, the girl returned, the duke in tow. He entered the sick room, took one look at Lord Highcliff and then at Effie. To Minerva, he said, "You required my assistance?"

"Miss Darrow has been looking after Lord Highcliff much to her own detriment. I fear she is too weak now to make it safely to another chamber on her own. Would you be kind enough to carry her?" Minerva asked. She uttered all of it without looking at him. She couldn't.

Effie immediately protested. "That is not necessary—"

"Miss Darrow," the duke said gently. "Forgive me for saying this as we are not well acquainted, but it is very apparent that you have cared for Highcliff until you are on the verge of collapse. As a show of my gratitude for your care of an old and dear friend, please allow me to assist you."

It was uttered so prettily that even Minerva could not find fault with it. And when Effie gave a curt nod, she was too relieved to hold on to the full force of her anger. It settled within her to a mild resentment. When the younger student showed the duke out, Effie cradled gently in his arms, Minerva took up Effie's vigil at Highcliff's bedside.

She could certainly understand Effie's fascination with the man. His features were finely carved, like a work of art. But it wasn't just his handsomeness that lured women to him. It was the element of danger that seemed to ooze from him, like a wounded animal that one wished to aid, but that might very well lash out at any moment.

As if her thought had conjured deed, Highcliff jerked awake in that moment. Eyes blazing, he turned toward her, but it was obvious he did not see her. Whatever demons lurked in his very shadowy past, they were clearly tormenting him in that moment. He reached out, grasping her arm and twisting her wrist painfully.

"Where is Effie? What did you do with her?"

"Effie went to rest. She's been caring for you for several days. She will make herself ill if she does not rest." Minerva uttered the words as calmly as possible, trying not to react to the biting pain in her arm.

"You lie. She would not leave me. Never," he said, though there was doubt in his gaze. "If she was ever really here."

"Lord Highcliff, you are at the Darrow School. You've been injured," Minerva said, trying to jog his memory. But it was no use. She saw his eyes cloud over with confusion and then he was lunging at her.

The chair toppled backward and he came out of the bed after her, landing on top of her. His hands gripped her throat. Minerva struggled, clawing at his hands to free herself, but for a man so gravely ill, his strength was shocking.

"I won't die here. I won't die in this hellhole!" he shouted.

Her vision was beginning to dim. Minerva continued to paw at his hands, but her efforts were becoming slower and even more ineffective as the loss of air began robbing her of strength.

When she thought it was too late, when she realized she might very well die at the hands of a man who truly—in his right mind—would never have meant her harm, his hands were suddenly pulled free and the rush of air left her coughing violently. Sitting up, she scrambled back toward the door as the duke wrestled Lord Highcliff back into the bed.

"Highcliff," he said sharply. "It's me! It's Hargrieve... it's Barrett!"

Highcliff stopped struggling then, his side wet with blood as he stared up at the man who'd just bested him. "Barrett? Why are you here?"

"I've been looking for you. I needed your help... not as much, it appears, as you need mine."

Then the duke looked away from Highcliff and looked at her. The question was quite clear in his eyes. He wanted reassurance that she was well. Wincing a bit with pain, Minerva managed a nod. Then with as much dignity as possible, she got up off the floor and righted the overturned chair. She seated herself in it, but much further from Lord Highcliff's bedside than she had been before. That was a mistake she would not make again.

Chapter Fifteen

B ARRETT STARED DOWN at Highcliff in horror. Had he not been informed of the man's identity, he would not have immediately recognized him. This was not the dandy who flitted in and out of London parties and was the darling of every hostess of note. He was dirty, unshaven, pallid with hollow eyes and sunken cheeks. But for the moment at least, he was resting quietly.

"How long has he been here?" he asked softly, trying not to disturb the man.

"Several days at least. Mrs. Wheaton would know. I'm certain you could ask her," Minerva answered. Her voice was hoarse, a testament to just how close she had come to losing her life at Highcliff's hands earlier.

"I do not think your Mrs. Wheaton cares for me," he replied. His tone was light, an attempt to stave off the rush of emotion he felt. Still, Barrett's hands were clenched into fists at his sides. He'd never known such fear as when he saw her on the floor, her face turning blue as she struggled to free herself from the fevered man's grasp.

She smiled as he'd intended. "Mrs. Wheaton doesn't care for anyone of the male gender, I'm afraid. She's never divulged anything to us about her former life, but I strongly suspect that Mr. Wheaton was not an ideal husband."

Barrett nodded, leaving it at that. His gaze strayed to the red marks about Minerva's throat. They would bruise, he thought. She'd bear those marks for some time. "How badly are you hurt? Tell me the truth."

"I'm a bit sore," she admitted. "But it isn't unbearable. It was very frightening though and I am incredibly grateful that you were here to intervene."

Barrett looked away from her. He didn't want her gratitude. The very notion of it left him feeling frustrated and angry. Instead, he focused on something more pressing. "I will be sending for two strong footmen to assist with Highcliff's care. Miss Darrow cannot do it alone. She's exhausted herself to the point of illness. And after today's occurrence, it is quite obvious that Highcliff's mind is so twisted by fever and injury that he cannot be cared for by anyone else he might overpower."

Minerva frowned at him. "Where are you going?"

"I cannot wait for Highcliff's assistance. I must go to Bedlam and see if I can get John released into my care," he stated. The longer he delayed, the more the child would suffer. That could not stand.

"I should go with you. If the boy is frightened... well, most of the employees there are men. He might be less inclined to be combative or to be so terribly fearful if there is a woman present."

He shook his head. "As capable as you are, Miss Stone, even you cannot be in two places at once. And you are needed here. Miss Darrow cannot care for him alone. Not anymore. She's too weak by far and he's clearly not out of the woods yet. Highcliff is a man to whom I owe a considerable debt. It would mean a great deal to me to know that you are helping to care for him... though you certainly will not be doing so alone."

Minerva stared at him for a moment. "What was it like?"

"What?"

"Bedlam," she stated. "What was it like in there?"

He'd never talked about that with anyone. In fact, he'd always sworn that he never would. The horrors of that place were something he longed to forget. But it wasn't morbid curiosity or even pity that had prompted her to ask. He could see it in her gaze—her concern for him, her fear that what he had to do might bring back painful memories. The truth, quite simply, was that those memories never went away. They were with him every hour of every day. "It's a kind of hell that defies description," he admitted. "If you are not mad when you go in, you will likely be when you leave it. They rob you of all the things that make you human. They take your name, your self-respect, your basic dignity—you are left with nothing but misery, humiliation, and impotent fury. Because you cannot fight back. You cannot defend yourself against anything that anyone in there wishes to do to you. The very act of defending yourself marks you as a violent lunatic. Meanwhile, the act of tolerating their abuses marks you as someone so lacking basic intellect that you will not defend yourself. In short, they create a horrid situation in which you are truly damned no matter what path you choose."

She looked away, swallowing convulsively. "And no doubt such an environment draws the worst sort of people to work there. When people desire to be cruel, and many do, the lure of such a population with no power to fight back or protest must surely be too great to resist."

"Precisely, Miss Stone. It is a breeding ground for cruelty and abuse."

"Bring him here," she suggested. "You saw Mrs. Wheaton with Meredith. That woman, despite her gruffness with you, is precisely what any child who has been treated so cruelly would need. It will do him all the good in the world. And her, too, I think."

He could not commit to that, not until he knew more about the boy's condition. "I will consider it. If it is possible, I will do so. But until I see him, until I can discern what has been done to him, I cannot make that promise."

"You will be careful." She uttered it as a statement of fact rather than a question or instruction.

"Yes. I will be careful. And so will you. I will sit with Highcliff for a moment. You will go downstairs and send a note to Sissy to send over two footmen. I cannot leave here if I do not know you are safe."

Minerva rose. She started to say something further to him, but then thought better of it. Instead, she simply nodded and left the room. Alone with only Highcliff, who had slipped into a fitful slumber, Barrett watched her go. He knew a moment of regret for all the things that could never be between them. He wanted to be selfish—to claim her regardless of the fact that she deserved so much more. But that would make him the monster others already accused him of being.

Muttering a curse under his breath, he moved away from the bed and looked out the window to the small, barren garden below.

"Only a woman can make a man so miserable."

The hoarsely rasped observation had come from Highcliff who was apparently not sleeping, after all.

"I thought you were hovering too close to death's door to be bothered by my melancholia," Barrett intoned dryly.

Highcliff gave a weak, bitter chuckle. "Just commiserating with a similarly afflicted fellow. Women will drive you to the brink of insanity and then smile when they push you over the edge."

Truer words had never been spoken.

DOWNSTAIRS, MINERVA MADE her way to Effie's small study. She would send the note to Sissy and secure the necessary footmen to assist with Lord Highcliff's care. She certainly had no wish to repeat the events that had transpired earlier.

Lifting one hand to her bruised throat, Minerva winced as she encountered the tender bruises that were beginning to form there. If Barrett—the duke, she corrected—had not returned when he did, things would have gone very differently. Highcliff, delirious as he was, might well have killed her. It would have been a tragic accident but Effie would never have forgiven herself for it and any chance of ever putting things right between the two of them would have been gone forever.

Dashing off the note, she left the study and found Mrs. Wheaton overseeing two of the girls who were currently on punishment duty as they cleared the dining quarters of the breakfast dishes. "Mrs. Wheaton, where is Meredith?"

"In class, dear. I thought it might be good for her to go to classes with the younger girls. She was quite excited at the prospect."

Considering that Meredith's studies had been quite neglected with all their traveling, Minerva felt some small degree of relief at that statement. "That was an excellent notion, Mrs. Wheaton. Thank you."

"You're in love with him," the older woman accused.

Minerva pasted a slightly puzzled smile on her face. "I don't know what you mean."

"The duke," Mrs. Wheaton scoffed. "You're in love with him. My eyes are not so old that they have gone blind with it."

"I am not in love with anyone."

"You can lie to yourself, Missy, but you cannot lie to me. Known you since you weren't any bigger than that child who came here with you today! I saw the way you looked at him... and I saw the way he looked at you. You're playing with fire."

Minerva looked away then. "Whatever our feelings, Mrs. Wheaton, the duke and I are both well aware that nothing can come of them."

"And where is he now?"

"There was an incident with Lord Highcliff. He was quite delirious and did not know what he was doing... but he was very violent. The duke has asked that I send a note to his great-aunt to have two footmen sent over to help with his care until he is himself again," she replied.

Mrs. Wheaton stepped closer to her. Then she began to cluck her tongue. "He nearly throttled you!"

"Yes. He did. But luckily, the duke was here and intervened. Now, can you get one of those miscreant boys that loiter outside the Hound's place of business to deliver this missive?"

"I can," Mrs. Wheaton said. "But you'll sit down in the kitchen and let me tend those bruises as soon as I'm done."

As it would spare her having to return upstairs and see the duke once more before he left for Bedlam to retrieve his cousin and heir, she would gladly comply with that edict.

Moments later, Mrs. Wheaton was bustling into the kitchen as Minerva patiently waited for her. While the housekeeper gathered her various cures and remedies, Minerva couldn't help but think of the many times she'd sat in that same spot to have various ailments and injuries cared for.

As Mrs. Wheaton returned and began laying out her assorted supplies, the housekeeper stated, "I know what they say about him. About what they say he did as a lad."

Minerva nodded. "I know what they say, too. But it isn't true. You have only to spend any time with him at all to know that."

The housekeeper nodded. "He won't marry you though. Not a duke. And not a duke who is already mired in scandal. He'll need to make a respectable marriage—and while I love you, child, we both know where you come from and that won't ever be up to snuff for someone in his straits."

It hurt to have her own thoughts echoed back at her by another. Nonetheless, she gave a slight nod. "I know that, too."

Mrs. Wheaton nodded then. "Then let's get you all fixed up, hmm?"

Minerva smiled and let the older woman treat her scrapes and bruises. There were some hurts that nothing would heal, however.

꧁꧂

CHARLOTTE WAITED IN the drawing room of the supposedly ruined house. It still reeked of smoke, but otherwise was habitable. It goaded her beyond belief that Barrett had the gall to snoop through the house to confirm it. Oh, she longed for the day when he would no longer be a thorn in her side.

As the door opened and her scapegrace sons entered, she surveyed their bruised and battered appearance. Normally, she indulged them because it simply made life easier. But she'd never been more disappointed in them than she was at that moment.

"Look at the pair of you! You're both an absolute mess. If anyone sees you there will be talk and if there is talk, Barrett will hear of it. How difficult will it be for him to piece it all together? His two cousins are black and blue from a brawl and he was set upon by two masked footpads he thoroughly trounced! You might as well have signed a confession and slipped it into his pocket," she accused.

"I'm sorry, Mother," Willis murmured. "I did not realize he would be so handy with a sword. I was outmatched and could not best him."

"I was outmatched and could not best him," she mocked. "I'm well aware of that, Willis! And you, Peter! For all your talk of hating him so much and wanting to teach him a lesson! He knocked you on your arse and left you there, didn't he? You're both as worthless as your stepfather was! Need I remind you what is at stake here?"

They both shook their heads.

Despite their denial, Charlotte continued. "Unless you want to live in penury forever, restricted to what he says we may have, he must die. When he is gone, we will retrieve your idiot brother from Bedlam and the de facto dukedom will be yours... along with all that glorious wealth."

"We will try again, Mother," Willis vowed. "And we will not

fail this time."

"No," she said. "It's too risky. If he were to identify either of you, it would be over before it began. No. We will take funds we cannot afford to part with and hire someone to do the deed. I know just the man."

"It isn't as if we're the only ones who failed," Peter blurted out suddenly. "Your original plot to kill him as a boy is the reason we're still having to deal with him today!"

Charlotte rose and crossed the room to where her younger son stood. Without hesitation, she drew her hand back and slapped him hard enough to split his lip. He glared daggers back at her, but his fists remained clenched at his side. He was smart enough, despite his wicked and unpredictable temper, not to test her. Charlotte had no sentimentality about motherhood or anything else. Her children had always been a means to an end for her. The eldest two had kept her first husband happy enough and generous enough until the poison she'd slowly fed him had finally ended his miserable life. Meredith and the embarrassment of her youngest son had kept Barrett's uncle in check. Her sons had been serving a purpose. They'd been given one single task... to kill their cousin and make it look like an accident. Once in town, they had more leeway to even make it look like a robbery by footpads. But they'd failed her at every turn. If she had to hang them out to dry to save herself, she would.

"Do not test me, Peter. There are mothers in the wild who will eat their young... and they are not as vicious or cold-hearted as I am," she warned him.

He didn't meet her gaze. Instead, he focused his eyes on some point past her shoulder and simply mumbled, "Yes, Mother."

Chapter Sixteen

THE SMELL ASSAULTED him first. Urine, unwashed bodies, sickness and general uncleanliness—it filled the air and made the bile rise in his throat. The sounds were painfully familiar as well. Distant wailing, profanities spewed in rapid-fire speech by pacing, manic inmates and the annoyed, warning shouts of the guards for them to shut their mouths. In all the years since he'd been freed from this place, if anyone ever truly was freed from it, nothing had changed.

"I need to speak to the administrator of this facility," he said to the guard as he entered.

"Who are you to demand a meeting, then?"

"I am the Duke of Hargrieve," Barrett said. "And you will inform him that I am here or I will have your job before the next hour strikes!"

The guard sneered, but walked away to speak to someone. One of the other employees looked in his direction for a moment, narrowed his eyes, and then headed off down the corridor, presumably to inquire if he could see the man in charge of the hellish nightmare.

A few moments later, that same man returned and beckoned for him to follow. It felt impossibly strange to walk willingly into the depths of that building. The further he traveled along those corridors, the more the hair on his nape rose as he felt the outside world slipping away. It would be so easy to get lost in there forever, to have a locked door take him away once more from everything he held dear. Minerva's face suddenly appeared in his mind. She was dearer to him than anything, even though he barely knew her, even though she was entirely forbidden to him.

They emerged from one corridor lined with dirty cells into another that was swept clean and well lit. Toward the end of that corridor was a series of offices. He recognized them. That was where he'd been brought to Highcliff when he'd finally been discharged as a patient of the Bethlem Hospital.

Entering the last office, he faced a man who was not unknown to him. It was the very same man who'd held him prisoner there, who'd allowed Charlotte and his uncle to lock him away without cause.

"Ah... it's you. You're certainly taller than you were when last we met," the man chuckled.

"And far less easily intimidated... I am a duke, after all. And wealthy enough despite my tattered reputation to have you removed from your post."

The man frowned then. "Speak your peace, Hargrieve. This is a place for working men."

"John Graves. I want him discharged into my custody," Barrett said.

"I'm afraid I cannot do that... the boy's mother has entrusted me with his care—"

"The boy's mother is a scheming bitch," Barrett replied. "You will release him to me or I will have you removed from your post. Not only that, but I will see to it that you are never again employed in any capacity that will allow you to earn more than a pittance. The boy. Now."

"You cannot just make these demands!"

"I can. I have. And they will be met. Get him or so help me you will regret it," Barrett vowed. Apparently his tone was very persuasive. The man rang a bell on his desk and an attendant appeared. Instructions were given and then they waited in silence.

The man's anger and resentment were palpable. Barrett did not care. He was half-tempted to have the lout fired anyway. He was a worthless sot who abused women and children alike. He treated the female inmates as his own private stable and the children as little more than the sand bags used for pugilistic lessons at Gentleman Jack's.

It seemed to take an interminable amount of time before the attendant returned with a small boy in tow. He was skin and bone, his complexion pale with large, dark hollows beneath his eyes. In short, he looked like the prisoner he was.

"Hello," Barrett said.

The boy did not speak, but he did look up at him. His expression was guarded and cautious.

Barrett stooped down so they were eye to eye. "Hello, John. I'm your cousin. My name is Barrett and I've come to take you away from this place. Would you like to leave here?"

The little boy said nothing, but his gaze darted to the window and the pale sunlight that was filtering in from outside. He might not speak, but it was quite clear to Barrett that he understood every word.

Barrett reached out, but the boy flinched away from his touch. Swallowing the rage that incited him, Barrett tried again, this time extending his hand palm up. "Take my hand, John. We will walk out of here together. I will take you to a nice place where a very friendly lady will cook you a wonderful meal. You will be given a bath, clean clothes and you will sleep in a bed that is just yours with fresh, clean linens and no one to harm you ever again. I promise that to you here and now."

The administrator chuckled, a mean and derisive sound. "Promise all you want! You'll bring him back here before the month is out! The boy is not fit for anything but the asylum. He's been here for almost five years and has never spoken a word in all that time."

"Do not listen to him. He's a liar. We both know that," Barrett said, keeping his voice soft and calm.

The little boy reached out then, placing his grimy hand in Barrett's. And then he looked up, past Barrett and to the man who was seated behind the desk laughing at him. He opened his mouth, and the sound that emerged from it was rough, but it was a voice. "B-ba-bastard."

Barrett grinned at the young boy. "That, John, was a perfect choice for your first word. Let's leave this place."

EFFIE AWOKE LATE that afternoon and returned to her chamber which had been transformed into Highcliff's sick room. Her surprise at finding a footman parked outside the door was apparent. "What is this all about?"

Minerva braced herself to share the tale of her earlier encounter with the injured lord. It would trouble Effie. It would also inspire guilt when it was quite clear that her friend and mentor was troubled enough. "There was an incident earlier. Lord Highcliff, in his delirium—well, there is no way to say it that will not be unpleasant. He attacked me. Had the duke not been here, I daresay things would have ended very poorly. As the duke had other matters today that he had to attend to, he sent over two footmen that will work in twelve hour shifts so that such an event will never be repeated... not for anyone who happens to be caring for Lord Highcliff at that time."

Effie walked toward her, placed one hand under Minerva's chin and tipped her head back. The gesture revealed the ugly bruises that had already begun to form around her throat— bruises that were unmistakably a man's handprints. "I have much to thank his grace for. If he were himself, Highcliff would never have harmed you."

"I know. It truly was not his fault. He is a man very haunted by the events of his past, I think. And right now, with his mind so befuddled by fever, he is at the mercy of those difficult memories," Minerva replied. "I harbor no ill will toward him over this incident. But, tell me the truth, Effie... are there other things that warrant harboring a grudge against him?"

Effie turned away then, moving to Highcliff's bedside where she smoothed the sheets over him and rested the back of her hand against his forehead. "He feels cooler, I think. Perhaps the fever will break soon."

It was blatant avoidance. Minerva tried a different tack. "He hurt you. Not physically. He wounded your heart."

Effie glanced back over her shoulder at Minerva wearing the saddest of smiles. "We wounded each other. Neither of us is married. Yet, neither of us is free. I love him... I love him too much to ever marry another. And he is too noble to marry me when he sees himself as so much less than he really is. He has this ridiculous notion that I deserve better."

"Do you really believe that is his reason? Something so noble and yet so terribly misguided?" Minerva couldn't fathom it.

"I know him, Minerva. Better, I think, than he knows himself. There are very few secrets between us... well, personal secrets. There are things he has done, things that he continues to do for king and country that I will never be privy to. And that is as it should be. But yes, I believe it with my whole heart. He has never known his worth because the people who should have shown it to him were incapable. All he received from his father was cruelty and cold neglect. But I don't wish to discuss Highcliff anymore. Certainly not with him lying here likely listening to the whole of it. I'd much rather discuss the duke. What precisely, Minerva, is happening between the two of you?"

"Am I wearing a sign? How is that everyone I encounter seems to suspect that something untoward has occurred between me and the duke?" Even as she asked the question, Minerva's cheeks were flushing with embarrassment.

"Did it?"

"It was a kiss, Effie. One kiss. And we both agreed that it was a terrible error in judgment and would not be repeated," Minerva admitted. Saying it out loud, that the gloriousness of being in his arms and having him kiss her was gone forever made her want to weep. Never before had she resented her ignoble birth quite so much.

"If there is one thing I know, kisses have a tendency to alter things irrevocably. It cannot be undone, you see? Now that you both know, now that forbidden fruit has been savored, it will always be there between you," Effie replied. "So you must ask yourself, truthfully, if you are capable of keeping that vow."

Minerva straightened her shoulders and stiffened her spine. "I must be. The alternative, of becoming his mistress—or worse, a simple dalliance—I will not do that. I cannot sacrifice everything I am for so little. I considered it. But I am not my mother. I am not going to content myself with a man whom I would have to share. The cost of being his dirty secret would be too great."

Effie nodded as she settled herself on the edge of the bed next to the man who presented the very same quandary for her. "I understand that all too well. You cannot continue to work for him. Not if you mean to keep that promise to yourself."

"I cannot leave Meredith. Not now. Not so soon after her mother abandoned her, too."

"Then be prepared for what will happen." Effie's warning was uttered softly, with no judgment, but profound sadness and no small degree of empathy.

A knock sounded on the door and then Mrs. Wheaton bustled in. "His grace has returned, Miss... with the boy. It'll fair break your heart."

Minerva rose. "I have to go, Effie."

"Think about what I've said."

Minerva met Effie's worried gaze and nodded. "As if I have a choice in the matter... I will return later."

Chapter Seventeen

MEREDITH WAS HOVERING near the doors to the drawing room. Several other students were hanging back, tucked into a small alcove just beneath the stairs. All of them were focused so completely on the goings-on beyond those pocket doors that a cannon could well have gone off without anyone noticing.

Minerva walked past where Meredith stood and rounded the bend to address the gathered students. "This is a private family matter for Meredith and the duke. You will not eavesdrop. The lot of you are to return to your rooms or go to the kitchens and be given a task to keep you occupied."

There were some grumbled responses to that directive. But after a moment, the girls wandered away to do as they'd been instructed.

Once the corridor was clear, Minerva walked back to where Meredith stood, peeking in through the pocket doors. "Do you want to go in?"

"I'm not certain. Will he remember me, do you think?"

Minerva shrugged. "I cannot say. He was very small when your mother sent him away. He might. But if he does not, you have the opportunity to start fresh with him."

"I want a real brother," Meredith said. "Mother doesn't really like me... she doesn't like any of us. Peter is mean and Willis just doesn't care. I want a real family. Am I wicked for saying so?"

Minerva felt her heart breaking for the very lonely child at her side. Perhaps her suffering had not been as overt as that which her brother had been subjected to, but she was no less wounded for it. She felt unloved, unwanted and utterly alone. How on earth could she ever leave the duke's employ and abandon Meredith when so many others had already done so? No matter what it cost her personally, she couldn't do it. She could not be one more disappointment in the child's life. "No, Meredith, I do not think that is wrong at all. But you won't find it by lingering in the corridor. You must go and face him."

Meredith raised a trembling hand, not to the door, but to clutch at Minerva's hand. Then she gave a sharp nod signifying that she was ready.

Minerva lifted her hand and knocked softly. After a brief hesitation, the duke spoke, urging them to enter. Parting the polished wooden doors, she stepped into the drawing room with Meredith at her side.

"Meredith," the duke said, "This is your brother, John."

"I know," the little girl replied. "I remember him. Do you remember me, John?"

The little boy, dirty and unkempt, with what appeared to be a layer of bruises beneath the grime simply stared wide-eyed at Meredith for the longest moment. Then, without warning, he sprang from the settee and shot forward toward his sister. Minerva wanted to shield her, to protect her. But before she could react, it became abundantly clear that it wasn't necessary. The little boy simply wrapped his arms around what must have been the first familiar person he'd encountered. He hugged his sister so tight and so desperately and he began to sob. Great shudders wracked him. His shoulders quaked with the force of it. And Meredith simply sank to the floor with him, holding him as he wept.

Minerva could feel the tears flowing freely over her own cheeks. How could anyone viewing such a scene not weep?

Trying to recover, to pull herself together, she looked away and found the duke staring at those two children—siblings he had reunited—but it wasn't sadness she saw in his gaze. It was fury. In that moment, she could almost pity Mrs. Entwhistle-Graves. The woman had no idea what her machinations had unleashed.

BARRETT WATCHED THE display in front of him, the two heartbroken children, and all he wanted to do was throttle Charlotte. He would not lie to himself and say that it was purely altruistic. His anger and fury wasn't sparked only by what they had endured though that was certainly enough to warrant it. No. He could clearly recall the impotent rage, the fear, the sheer injustice of it all when she had sent him to that hellhole.

His uncle had not been blameless in the matter but it had always been perfectly clear to him and anyone else who saw the couple interact that Charlotte was the one in charge. It was never a question that his uncle would defer to her in all things. Sending him to Bedlam had been Charlotte's plan all along. From the moment he had entered their home—still suffering terrible, debilitating headaches following his injury, along with the lapses in his memory from the time of attack—she had pressed his uncle to have him committed. She'd gone into endless hysterics about how they could all be murdered in their beds by him. And always, those lamentations had been uttered in front of others, further cementing the possibility that he might be guilty of the crime.

In truth, Charlotte was wholly responsible for all of society believing him a murderer. Given his age and his own injuries at the time, few would have even considered it a possibility if she had not brought it to light. Whatever reason she'd had, she had cast doubt upon him. So much so that there were moments when even he had questioned whether or not he was capable of such despicable acts.

Then she'd locked him away. Men from Bedlam, along with that damned administrator, had come to the London house to collect him. They'd carted him away kicking and screaming with terror blooming in his chest.

The cold, damp cells; the meals that were little better than slop; the predatory nature of other inmates who would have used and abused him in terrible ways if not for the kindness of others who had protected him—all of that could be laid squarely at Charlotte's feet. And then she'd done the same thing to her youngest child. Why?

What possible purpose did she have?

"Meredith, I think John might feel better once he's had a bath and had something to eat. Why don't you take him to Mrs. Wheaton and let her get him settled?" Minerva suggested softly.

Her voice, soft and so very soothing, penetrated the haze of his anger. Then the children were leaving the room, Meredith holding one of her brother's hands. His other hand was locked firmly on her skirts, almost as if he feared letting go of her lest she disappear from his life again. It was painful to observe. It also brought firmly into focus what his primary objectives should be. He could not undo any part of his past. It would never go away. But he could take the necessary steps to ensure that Charlotte could never do something like that to that poor boy ever again. He had to protect them. No matter the cost.

Barrett could feel her looking at him, the weight of her concern almost a tangible thing. He lifted his head, their gazes locking. "Yes?"

"You are not well," she said.

"No," he admitted. "I am not. Going back to that place has made me recall very vivid things I desperately wished to forget. But that is unimportant in the overall scheme of things, is it not? John is here, reunited with his sister and, hopefully, he is young enough and resilient enough that he will be able to put this terrible experience behind him."

"Two years. Two years of torment I cannot even imagine...

and he's so very small. I can only think that the asylum is very similar to the workhouse in the way its inhabitants must compete with one another for warmth, food, comfort."

"How would you know those things?" he demanded.

"A very dear friend of mine... Calliope, now the Countess of Montgomery, spent much of her childhood in one of those terrible places. She spoke of it very rarely, but she did confide in me at times about the terrible things she endured there." As she spoke, Minerva moved through the room, coming to a halt before the windows where she looked out into the street. "I doubt very seriously that Mrs. Entwhistle-Graves provided extra funds to see to the boy's comfort. Just as I am sure she did not do so for you."

He laughed bitterly at that. "Charlotte cares little for anyone's comfort but her own. No, she did not take any measures to see to our care beyond paying the basic fees to have us both locked away. I should speak to Mrs. Wheaton. He will eat until he makes himself sick if he is permitted."

Minerva shook her head. "You needn't. Mrs. Wheaton has dealt with all manner of abuses and neglect with the children who have come through this door. She will know just what to do for him."

Wanting to change the subject, needing to distract himself from talk of Bedlam and all its horrors, he asked, "How is Highcliff?"

"Slightly improved. His fever seems to be lessening, or so Effie says. It may only be wishful thinking on her part. Thank you for your help... both with the incident upstairs and providing the footmen. I will rest much easier knowing that Effie has someone to aid her should he have another episode."

His gaze roamed over her, taking in the scrapes on her hands, the bruises at her throat. That she could remain so calm and so concerned for others in the face of what had very nearly happened to her left him feeling strangely angry at her. He wanted to shake her, wanted to demand that she leave and let

Miss Darrow deal with her own problems.

"But, I've decided, for Meredith's sake and now for John's, that we should return to Sissy's. I think they need time to rebuild their bond and there are too many prying eyes in this place. The girls mean well, but they are all terribly nosy," she admitted with a rueful grin. "I have asked some of Effie's other former students to provide support by helping her to care for Highcliff. Most of them owe him some degree of gratitude for his assistance in difficulties they or their respective husbands have faced. So, I think they will be glad to help."

It was an instant relief. In an effort to lighten the mood and the conversation, he asked, "Do you think we could bribe Mrs. Wheaton to come with us? I'd do just about anything to see her take Charlotte down a peg or two."

Minerva grinned at that. "As would I, I think. But now, there is no power on earth that could tempt her from Effie's side. She is entirely devoted."

He didn't intend to say it. There was no warning as he simply opened his mouth and the words fell out. "Last night in the library... what happened between us—"

"We both agreed that was a mistake and will not happen again," she said quickly.

"No. You said it was a mistake. You said it should not happen again. Mistake or not, Minerva, it will happen. There is something between us that I have never experienced before. From the moment I first saw you, I have been unable to get you out of my mind. You invade my thoughts, both waking and asleep. And the more I fight it, the more futile it seems. For it is a battle I cannot win." He paused then just to draw a breath before admitting, "Further, I'm not certain I want to."

"That isn't entirely your decision to make," she stated, her tone haughty.

He'd irritated her, he thought, surprisingly pleased by the fact. As she'd robbed him of any sense of peace or calm from the moment she'd first crossed the threshold of his home, it was a rather satisfying tit for tat.

Getting to his feet, he crossed from the settee to where she stood. "I'll never force you to do anything. We both know that. But do not pretend that you are unmoved by me. We both know that is a lie. Or should I remind you that I offered you the chance to tell me to stop last night and you refused. You begged me to kiss you. And you will again. Because this... whatever it is between us, is inevitable. Neither of us can deny or avoid it, however we might wish to."

Chapter Eighteen

T HE GOOSE AND Garters was not a reputable establishment. As far as inns or taverns in London were concerned, it ranked only slightly above sleeping on the street. With a heavy cloak covering her from head to toe, her identity concealed beneath the deep hood, Charlotte entered the establishment. She had a single coin clutched in her palm. When she approached the bar, she placed the coin on the scarred wood and tapped her finger on it to draw the innkeeper's eyes.

"We don't serve sherry," he sneered.

"I'm looking for Martin Pfife," she said, ignoring the man's quip. "The coin is yours if you point me in his direction."

The innkeeper eyed her coolly. "If it's a husband you want done in, there are men what will do it cheaper than Pfife."

"Pfife comes highly recommended. Where is he?"

The innkeeper reached out and placed the tip of his finger on the coin next to hers. "That corner in the back," he said, jerking his head toward a single table cloaked almost entirely in deep shadow. "That's his. You take a seat there and he'll come find you."

Charlotte let go of the coin, watching as the man slid it across the bar top, picked it up and then bit it between his few remaining teeth to check that it was real. Disgusted by him and her surroundings, she nonetheless made her way back to the table in that darkened corner and seated herself. She'd wait for however long it took until Pfife arrived. After all, he'd failed in his duties the first time. It was only right that he should complete the job.

It was only moments later that a man got up from another table in the tap room and made his way back to her. He was a large man, broad-shouldered and raw-boned. His hair was mostly silver, his face heavily lined and he was none too cleaned. But as he seated himself across from her, she could not suppress a shiver. There was a coldness in his gaze, a calculating air about him that told her he was most certainly the man she'd come looking for. He was a killer, a man capable of murder and that was precisely what she wanted done.

"I don't work cheap," he said. "But I gets it done."

Charlotte, beneath her hood, arched one eyebrow at him. Carefully, she pushed back her hood far enough that her face would be visible only to him. "That isn't always true. There is one instance in particular where the job most certainly did not 'get done', Mr. Pfife."

He scoffed. "Not bloody likely. I don't leave witnesses."

"But you did... a duke and his three sons. The youngest boy received a very nasty blow to the head that, by all rights, should have killed him. But fortune smiled on him that day." Charlotte watched his reaction. She saw the way his jaw tightened, his eyes narrowing with anger. Then she smiled.

"I trusted the wrong man to be my partner that day. 'e went soft because it was children."

"He isn't a child now," she replied. "Now he is the Duke of Hargrieve... and I need you, Mr. Pfife, to finish what you started."

He chuckled. "Weren't you that 'ired me, Missus. I won't be answering to you now, neither."

Charlotte smiled coolly. "You are so very wrong, Mr. Pfife. My husband may have paid you and delivered the instructions, but rest assured, he did so at my behest. I am willing to offer an added incentive to the original fee. Not what you would normally work for, but as this is extra work and a complication no one anticipated, I am willing to be generous."

"I don't think so. I'll be turning down this job," he said. "Don't need the trouble."

Charlotte clucked her tongue sadly. "I'm afraid that's not an option. You see, if you do not do what I ask of you, I will see to it that the current duke is informed of your identity. I promise you that he will leave no stone unturned until you are found and hanged for your crimes."

Pfife slapped his palms violently down on the table. "What's to stop me from killing you right now and putting a stop to it all?"

"Because I've left a note in the care of a trusted individual that identifies you as the man who murdered the former duke and his two eldest sons, attacking and leaving the youngest son for dead. If I fail to return home, that note will be delivered to the current duke. You see, Mr. Pfife, there is only one way to avoid paying for what you did… and that is to finish the job."

"Bitch!"

Charlotte knew then that she had won. Rising from the table, she said, "Get the job done, Mr. Pfife, then we can discuss your compensation. Good evening."

Victorious, Charlotte sailed out of the wretched little tavern and returned to her waiting hack. She was still smiling as she returned to the fire-damaged home in Mayfair.

IT WAS WELL beyond dark by the time they returned to Sissy's. Riding in the carriage with the duke, Meredith and John, silence reigned. No one spoke. The children simply huddled together, both of them seemingly content simply to be in one another's company. As for herself and the duke, things were still quite tense following their conversation in the drawing room. She resented him for what he'd said, primarily because it was true.

There was no small amount of shame in her. She had begged him to kiss her. He had offered to let her walk away and she had refused. Everything that had transpired between them in the library the night before had only happened because she had consented to it. Blaming him was unfair and dishonest—two things she prided herself on never being.

When the carriage came to a complete halt, the duke stepped out first. He helped John and Meredith down and ushered them toward the door before turning back to her. When he extended his hand to aid her, Minerva wanted desperately not to take it. It wasn't only her anger that prompted that response. Any touch between them terrified her because it might bring those feelings from the night before back to the surface when she had worked so diligently to tamp them all down.

"Do not be foolish, Miss Stone," he said. "It is dark and the pavement is uneven. If you fall, I will have no choice but to carry you inside. Take my hand. Despite what you may think of me, I am capable of being a gentleman."

"I am not a child to be scolded," she replied.

"If you were a child, Miss Stone, the complications currently between us would not be an issue," he replied just as sharply. "Take my hand."

Chastened and embarrassed, both by her behavior and the ridiculousness of their current situation, Minerva did as he demanded. She placed her hand in his and immediately felt the familiar jolt. It rocked her to her core and left her once more floundering to understand why he had such an effect on her when no other man ever had.

Once her feet were firmly on the ground, he let her go, but he remained close to her side as they climbed the steps to the ornate front door. Once inside, they looked at one another and simply parted ways. Minerva climbed the stairs to get the children settled into their beds for the night while he went the other direction and retreated to the library.

The entire incident only served to underscore the fact that

she was in an untenable situation. It was as if a clock were ticking away the minutes until she gave in to the overwhelming temptation of him. Resisting was surely a Sisyphean task.

Entering Meredith's room, she realized that there was little point in having had an additional room readied for John. Meredith was already tucked into her bed and John was on the floor next to it. She'd given him a pillow and a blanket but he used neither. His head swiveled toward her then, his eyes still wide open and not at all trusting. Meredith, however, was snoring softly.

"Won't you be cold?" she asked him in a whisper.

He shook his head.

"You're not very used to sleeping with blankets and pillows are you?"

Again, the little boy shook his head.

It was a chance, Minerva realized, for her to speak to him. He might not speak back, but he would answer her questions. To that end, she settled herself on the carpet near him. "May I ask you a few questions, John?"

He shrugged noncommittally.

Minerva didn't smile but the urge was there. She pursed her lips to hide it and then nodded as if she were giving her questions grave consideration. "Can you speak?"

He looked at Meredith and then at the door. Then he looked back at her and gave a short, brief nod.

"I see. Do you just choose not to speak?"

Another nod of his head.

"Is it difficult for you to speak?"

He nodded.

Minerva tried to conceal her excitement. "Do you stammer?"

He moved his hand a bit to show that he did a little.

"Do you struggle to find the words you want to say?"

There was a very enthusiastic nod to that question. In fact, he sat up and stared at her as if she were the first person to ever ask him about why he could not speak. Of course, given that his mother had no interest in any of her children and that Bedlam was simply a place to put people rather than heal them, she supposed that was very likely true.

"You know, John, there are ways that I might be able to help you with that. Would you like to try?"

Another nod, but more cautious.

"I will never scold you or punish you if you cannot say something," she offered. "We will simply try. And even if you can never say the words, I will teach you to read and write so that you will always be able to communicate with others. There are many ways, John, to get along in this world without ever talking at all. But we will do what we can to make it better for you."

Meredith had stopped snoring. She sat up in bed, leaned over the edge to look John directly in the eyes and said, "Miss Stone isn't like the people in that awful place, John. She will help you. I just know she will. She's ever so good."

In the face of that ringing endorsement, John looked at Minerva once more and then, with the merest whisper, uttered one small phrase. "H-help me."

"I will," Minerva vowed. And just like that, she knew she was never leaving the duke's employee. Come what may, she would stand by those two children no matter what.

Chapter Nineteen

B ARRETT LEFT THE house the following morning just after he'd broken his fast. Minerva was apparently having breakfast with the children in their room while she tried to teach Meredith's lessons and work with John on his speech. It goaded him that she was avoiding him to such a degree, but there was little he could do about it. After all, commanding her to spend time in his presence when she was actually performing the duties she had been hired for would make him precisely the sort of man he had always refused to be.

To salvage his pride and not beg for the scraps of her attention, he had elected to see to other matters. He needed some proof, beyond just his suspicion, that Charlotte was actually in town. Since it would be impossible for him to watch the house himself without being spotted, he would need to hire someone to do so. It would have been a much simpler prospect if Highcliff was conscious and lucid. So he resorted to a different solution. He took to the mews behind Sissy's house and spoke to a variety of stable lads. A few had brothers looking for work. Hiring young boys to watch the house would be far less suspect. After all, there were always children lingering in the better neighborhoods hoping to earn a coin by delivering missives or doing other errands.

Once that task was completed and arrangements had been

made for the house to be watched all hours of the day and night—with each boy having a description of Charlotte—he turned to the next item on his list. He would need to arrange for proper clothing for John and more clothing for Meredith as she had only a small valise with her. He had no notion what children would require but he could retain the services of a tailor and a dressmaker and send them to the house. It would deprive Sissy of shopping opportunities but, under the circumstances, without knowing what Charlotte was about or precisely where she was, it would be for the best. There was no predicting how she might respond when she discovered that John had been liberated from the asylum.

Making his way toward Bond Street, he became aware that someone was following him. Rather than glance over his shoulder and giving himself away, he found a small coffee house and stepped inside. Taking a seat at a table near the front window, he ordered a cup of coffee for himself and watched the street outside. After a few moments, a weathered-looking man in rough clothing walked by. He attempted to casually peer into the shop and then walked on past.

On the face of it, it was not unusual to see workmen in such clothing in that area. But there had been something in the man's demeanor which was off-putting. Not furtive, for he had been quite bold, but calculating perhaps. He was clearly there for a reason that had naught to do with an honest trade.

After the man was well past the shop, Barrett rose and stepped out into the street once more. He could see the man up ahead so he fell in step several yards back, keeping pace but staying within a crowd to avoid discovery. They began to tread very familiar territory. The man was going away from the shopping district and making his way back into the heart of Mayfair—back to the house where Sissy, Minerva and the children were currently residing. If there had been a single question in his mind that the man was following him, that put it to rest.

Was he some thug hired by Charlotte? Did he have something to do with the brick that had been thrown through the window the other night? There had been something familiar about him, Barrett reflected. A strange sense of déjà vu filled him. He couldn't place the man, but he felt certain that he'd seen him at some point before. It left him puzzled and unnerved. It also left him terribly worried for the few people in his life he did actually care for, all of whom were now under that same man's scrutiny.

Crossing the street, his pace quickened as he neared the house. He'd taken only two steps up the stone stairs leading to the front door when the shot rang out. He felt the wind of it as it passed him. Ducking down, he glanced behind him and saw the same man hurrying away, his hands buried in his coat pockets. He wanted to go after him, but he had no weapon on him in that moment. Without knowing whether or not the man had another pistol on him, it was too great a risk. Missing him might simply have been a lure. As the man disappeared into the park, heading directly for the thick cover of trees, it seemed likely.

There was too much at stake, he thought, to let temper lead him into a trap. Taking the remaining steps quickly, he let himself into the house to find the butler peering nervously through the sidelight.

"Your grace, are you injured?" the servant asked.

"No," Barrett replied. "The shot missed its mark. Are the children and Miss Stone still here? And my great-aunt?"

"Your great-aunt is in the morning room, your grace. Miss Stone has taken the children to the park. She thought some fresh air would do the boy some good."

Barrett didn't hesitate. He took the stairs two at a time until he reached his room. There, he gathered a brace of pistols and a knife. With the blade in his boot and a loaded and primed pistol in each coat pocket, he took the stairs at a run and left the house immediately.

Hyde Park was massive. He could only pray that he found Miss Stone and the children before someone else did—someone who might mean them harm.

MINERVA WATCHED HER charges carefully. The park was a bit crowded and she had been worried how all the people milling about might impact John. It seemed all her concerns were for naught. He barely noticed them. Instead, he sat in the grass, running his fingers back and forth over the tips of the blades, seemingly amazed by the texture and color of them.

Had going outside, touching something as simple as grass and feeling the sun on his face truly been denied him? The very thought of it made her want to weep. No child should ever be denied such basic joys.

A squeal of laughter had her turning her head and she saw a woman pushing a child in a pram while another child flew a kite a few yards ahead. It would likely be the last day they would have to enjoy the outdoors as the weather was unseasonably warm. The pram rolled past and her amusement at the sight of the exuberant infant faded as she saw a man standing just off the path, almost concealed beneath a copse of trees. She had seen him outside the house when they'd left to come to the park. Was he following them?

Unsettled now, she glanced back to where the children were. Meredith was twirling in the grass, giggling. It was the most childlike behavior she had ever exhibited. Another glance over her shoulder and the man was gone. Oddly, that did not make her feel better.

"Children," she said, drawing their attention as she rose to her feet and smoothed her skirts. "I know we've only been here a short time, but I think we should return home. Meredith, gather your things. John, come here to me, please."

"Must we go already?" Meredith asked.

"I'm afraid so. There is a matter that I must discuss with your cousin the duke." It wasn't really a lie, she reasoned. She certainly did mean to discuss the lurking stranger with him.

John walked toward her. He appeared more concerned than disappointed. But he immediately slipped his hand into hers.

Minerva stooped down to meet his gaze. "Did you see a man standing outside the house when we left this morning?"

The little boy nodded.

"Well, I saw that same man here in the park," Minerva stated. "He seems a bit suspicious to me and that is why we are going home. You haven't done anything wrong and this is not a punishment. Do you understand?"

He nodded, then glanced back at his sister who was dawdling in her task of collecting all her drawing supplies. Immediately, he removed his hand from hers and went to help Meredith with her things.

Minerva marveled at his intelligence, at his ability to adapt. But she worried about the dependence that was developing between the children. He needed interests and activities of his own. He needed *attachments*. Kept apart from the world for so long, he needed to find his place in it once more.

Once all their things were gathered, she ushered the children back along the path. She'd taken no more than a few steps when she heard a shout.

"Miss Stone! Miss Stone!"

Straight ahead was the duke. He was creating a terrible scene. But that did not anger her. It only intensified her earlier anxiety. For a man who detested bearing the brunt of gossip and rumors, to willfully draw attention to himself in such a way could only mean that something was horribly, horribly wrong. Hurrying her steps, she took one hand of each of the children, hastening them as well. When she was close enough that she would not have to scream, she asked very directly, "What is wrong?"

He kept walking, not halting his long strides until he was directly in front of her. "We must return home at once. It isn't safe here."

"To Aunt Sissy?" she asked.

"No... to Griffingate. As soon as it can be managed," he said. "Tomorrow at the latest."

Minerva looked at the children, both of whom had grown very tense during the exchange. "Let us get the children settled with Sissy and then we shall discuss it."

The duke looked down at the children's obviously frightened faces and said nothing more. He just gave a quick nod and then took up a position alongside Meredith. But during their walk, he scanned the park constantly, watching for any threat. It was no leisurely walk home, either. The pace was very quick, so quick in fact, that by the time they reached the house, Minerva found herself quite winded.

Sissy emerged from the morning room just then. "There you are! Come have some tea. Cook has made lovely scones."

"Miss Stone and I must have a word, Sissy," the duke replied. "Please take the children and get them a bite to eat." Even as he made the request, he was taking Minerva's arm and leading her to the drawing room.

Once they were closeted inside, he turned to her, "Did you see a strange man following you in the park?"

Minerva's heart sank. "I was hoping that was only my imagination... some strange paranoia. I saw him outside the house just as we were leaving. We had only been at the park for a few moments when I turned and saw him concealing himself inside the tree line. But it was unmistakable that he was there to observe us. Who is he?"

The duke walked away from her to peer out the window. "I wish I knew. He was following me on Bond Street. I ducked into a coffee shop to throw him off the scent, so to speak. When I emerged, I was following him... circuitously, of course. But it did not take long to realize what his destination was. When I arrived, he was leaving for the park. Presumably right behind you. When I asked the servants where you and the children were—only to be informed you were in the park, as well—I did not hesitate to come after you."

"You think Mrs. Entwhistle-Graves hired him," Minerva surmised.

"I cannot imagine who else would... I've never disclosed this to anyone else, Miss Stone, but I have long suspected that Charlotte had something to do with the death of my father and brothers. I have never had any proof. But she was so quick to cast aspersions on me. An act, I might add, which would leave her mired in scandal. Why would she do that unless it was to be certain that no one looked at either her or my uncle with suspicion?"

Minerva felt ill at the thought. She certainly held the woman in no great regard. But for her to be complicit to murder? Of course, she had been quite willing, it seemed, to turn a blind eye to rape. Was one really so far from the other on the scale of morality?

"What will you do if that is true?" she asked.

His jaw hardened. "I will see her punished in whatever way I can. My father and brothers deserve justice."

"And Meredith deserves to not grow up under the cloud of being born to a convicted murderer," Minerva said. "I am not unfeeling of your plight, nor am I unfeeling to the great injustice that was done to your family—but such a stain would likely see her ruined forever. Her future marital prospects would vanish entirely."

He whirled on her then, his fury unleashed in that moment. "Am I to sacrifice the blood shed by my family for a child I barely know?"

"A child who is now your dependent," she pointed out. "And what of John? His future is already uncertain at best. Until we can discern why it is that his speech is so inhibited and until we can begin to understand the depths of what he has suffered—he does not need another mark against him. Not if he is ever to take his rightful place in the world as your heir."

Some of the rage seemed to ease in him then. "I cannot let it simply go unpunished. If she is guilty—"

"If she is guilty she should pay, your grace," Minerva stated firmly. "But that punishment can be discreet. There are asylums, are there not? And as they have factored so keenly in all her schemes, it would be a fitting end for her, would it not? You want her to pay. I can think of no other way to make her suffer so greatly or for so long."

He stared at her for a long moment, his expression completely inscrutable. Then he simply shook his head. "You are as diabolical, Minerva Stone, as you are beautiful."

Chapter Twenty

IT SHOULD NOT have made her heart pound so fiercely in her chest. It should not have brought back, in startling relief, every second of their past encounters together. But it did all of that and so much more. She wanted desperately to step closer to him, to once more feel the strength and heat of him. She wanted to have him kiss her again with such passion and abandon that she lost all sense of morality and all sense of reason.

His pupils dilated, leaving his eyes almost entirely black. His nostrils flared as he inhaled sharply. And then that familiar tension was there between them, the aching awareness of one another that should have sent her running from the room. But it did not. Instead, she leaned into it, leaned into him—just close enough that their breaths mingled, their lips hovering scant inches from one another.

"It seems we are repeating our mistakes after all," he murmured.

"I can't help it," she admitted. "When I'm near you, it is all I can think of. Is it the same for you?"

"Morning, noon and night," he said. "Every waking minute and even in my dreams… you are inescapable."

She did not wait for him to kiss her. Not this time. Instead, she lifted slightly onto her toes and leaned in, placing her lips delicately over his. The scrape of his whiskers on her skin sent a shiver through her. The scent of him simply engulfed her and left her feeling dizzy with it, almost as if she were intoxicated by him. In a way, she supposed that was true.

As kissing went, she was hardly an expert. She'd been kissed a sum total of two times in her life and only one of those had she been a willing party to. Still, she managed. Moving her lips over his in the same fashion he had done when he'd kissed her only two days earlier, his response was unmistakable. His hands settled on the curve of her hips, his fingers tightening there, digging into her flesh with a kind of desperation that, while she did not truly understand it, she shared it. As close as they were—their lips locked together, their chests pressed together and their thighs bracketing one another—it was still not close enough. Too many layers, too many barriers between them.

His hands slipped into her hair, scattering pins as he angled her head back to deepen the kiss. She relished each second of it, letting him lead and coax her—not because she was unwilling, but because she was out of her depth. But she welcomed his touch, his tutelage. She wanted desperately to know what pleased him, to hope that she might be able to affect him as he affected her.

The kiss robbed her of all sense. When his hands began to roam—up from her hips to the small of her back, her shoulders, trailing lightly down over her ribs—that robbed her of breath. When he cupped one of her breasts in the palm of his hand, his thumb stroking over the pebbled peak, she sank against him, weak-kneed from that single touch.

And just like that, the moment ended. The door to the drawing room began to open and he pulled away quickly, crossing to the other window and standing with his back to the room.

There was no help for her hair, so Minerva simply twisted it into a quick knot and prayed whoever entered the room wouldn't notice. Of course, it was Sissy and since her primary goal was to see them together, she noticed. She noticed everything.

"This is rather cozy," she remarked. "The children are enjoying Cook's tea cakes and a bit of lemonade. They both seem to be none the worse for wear despite their ordeal. Would you care to explain to me precisely what that ordeal was?"

The duke turned only his head in Sissy's direction. "There was a man following me this morning... he looked quite familiar but I cannot place him. I lost him, and then doubled back to follow him. He led me here, eliminating any possibility that it was mere coincidence. As I was entering the house, he took a shot at me. It went wide, of course, missing me entirely but it certainly leaves no question as to his intent. I saw him vanish into the park and when I entered the house, I was informed that Miss Stone and the children had gone there for an outing."

"And you rushed to the rescue," Sissy surmised. "It's quite heroic, Barrett, but incredibly foolish. There are footmen, grooms, stable hands that you might have called on to accompany you. But no... you went off half-cocked and alone. Had he set a trap for you, you would have been rushing into it headlong!"

The racing of her heart, which had just calmed, picked up again, but for a very different reason. The very thought of him coming to harm filled Minerva with dread.

"What have you discovered about Charlotte?" Sissy demanded. "I know she is up to no good."

"On that point, Sissy, we are in complete agreement. The house is not damaged at all beyond a single room. A good airing and it would be habitable. Not to mention, I have every reason to think that Charlotte is right here in London, coming and going from a house that should be abandoned instead of socializing in Bath. I've set several boys to watch the house and report back should they catch sight of her," he remarked. "It is only a matter of time."

"That only proves her a liar," Minerva stated. "If she is responsible for this man who followed you and us... and made an attempt on your life, we still have no proof."

"We do not have it yet. But we will," he replied with far more confidence than she could lend credence to. "I intend to prove that Charlotte is guilty of this and so much more. For years, I have labored under the weight of rumors and gossip... it has controlled my life, prevented me from seeking a bride and living my own life. No more. I will be free of it and I will be free of her."

Sissy's eyebrows shot to her hairline as she let out a crow of victory. "You intend to take a wife! That is quite simply the most wonderful thing I have ever heard. It is high time you stopped living like a hermit... or a prisoner. You deserve some happiness, Barrett."

"I am not even certain I know what happiness is, Sissy... but I'm tired of letting her and all the rumors of my past control my life." His gaze left Sissy's and settled on Minerva. It was heated, filled with a kind of longing that left her weak and struggling for breath. "I should, at the very least, have the opportunity to pursue happiness, even if I do not find it or am incapable of feeling it."

"What will become of the children if their mother is found to be guilty of hiring this miscreant to carry out wicked deeds in her stead?" Sissy asked.

Barrett shrugged. "They are not their mother and will not be punished for the accident of their parentage. The children, Meredith and John, will remain with me. Peter and Willis will be given opportunities to secure their futures, but I will not let them reside in any of my homes... not when they have shown themselves capable of the same sort of villainy as their mother."

CHARLOTTE WAITED IN her carriage for her maid to return. She'd sent her into the market to find out any gossip she could from the duke's current abode, or any neighboring home. While the wide shot that had nearly taken him out was not exactly on everyone's lips, enough people were aware of it for the details to come back to her.

The maid returned, carrying a basket laden with fruit and bread they did not need. It was a guise, after all, an attempt to camouflage why they were there. But shopkeepers and vendors were quick to share tales with anyone who paid them for something.

"What did you find out?" Charlotte demanded.

The maid was huffing for breath. As portly as the middle-aged woman was, she'd moved quickly along the alleyway. She'd come to Charlotte a year ago, highly recommended by a friend for her ability to be discreet. Thus far, that was proving to be true. "No one saw the shooter," the maid said, gasping ever so slightly. "But his grace went in the house and returned moments later, with a brace of pistols and a knife. Headed into the park in pursuit. When he come out, there was no sign of the attacker but his grace was escorting the young governess and two children. Miss Meredith and a boy I did not recognize."

Charlotte's blood ran cold. "Two children?"

"Aye, Ma'am. A girl and a boy, younger and much smaller I think."

A boy. He'd found her secret. He knew about her son. Charlotte could feel panic clawing inside her. It was only a matter of time until everything else came out, she realized. If he had John in his custody—no, she thought. It wasn't possible. John would never be able to speak. The boy had been so terrified of her that he would never even try… assuming, of course, that he could remember anything that had occurred. Two years had passed since then and he'd been such a small child. The things he'd witnessed were, she hoped, gone forever.

But just to be sure, to be absolutely certain that her past sins had not come back to haunt her, she'd need to have another conversation with Mr. Pfife. There could be no more misses. His next shot would have to find its mark.

Banging on the roof of the hired hack with her parasol, she shouted, "Take me to The Goose and Garters!"

There was a moment of silence. No doubt the driver had

been so shocked he could not speak. After a moment, the man replied, "Yes, Ma'am. But I won't be staying there. You'll need another way back."

Chapter Twenty-One

BARRETT WAS IN his chamber. *Hiding.*

He hadn't intended to lose his head with Miss Stone again. It had never been his intent to kiss her. It certainly hadn't been his intent to boldly proclaim that, after years of denying himself any thought of companionship or affection in life, he had suddenly decided to take a wife. He had stopped short of stating that he intended to take her as his wife. After all, such a proclamation should be precipitated by a proposal and consent—neither of which had occurred as of yet.

Yanking at his loosely knotted craving, he tugged the offending garment away and tossed it onto a nearby chair. The poor man currently serving as his valet would likely have apoplexy when he saw it, but Barrett simply could not be bothered with those trivial trappings of civilization right now. He longed to be back in the countryside, walking his fields or riding, dressed like a farmer in rough clothing, only in shirtsleeves that could be rolled back in warmer weather. If he appeared like that in London, he could well find himself back in Bedlam. He was a duke, after all, and dukes were held to certain standards, whether he gave a damn about them or not.

If it wasn't for whatever would-be assassin Charlotte had likely hired, he'd go for a ride to clear his head. Thundering through the park did not offer the same sort of solace as riding over the fields at Griffingate, but it would still be a welcome respite from the perpetual temptation that was Miss Stone.

Over the course of the last day, he'd come to realize one particular fact that was unavoidable. She would haunt him. Every day of his life. Every night. She would be forever in his mind. There was only one cure and that was to have her. To stoke that flame until it burned out entirely.

On the surface, that was a simple enough solution. She obviously was as bedeviled by him as he was by her. Whatever force was drawing them together had not spared her any mercy either. But she was, whatever the circumstances of her birth or her position, very much a gently bred and gently reared young woman. He could not simply dishonor her by taking her virtue and then casting her aside. There were prices to be paid when one desired a woman to that degree and that woman was an innocent. Whatever others said of him, his honor would never allow him to ruin her and simply walk away. The question, in his mind, was whether or not she would consent to marriage.

During their relatively short acquaintance, he'd learned one thing about Minerva Stone that was irrefutable. She could be a maddening creature. Her temper could flare quickly but she was too proud to just state her feelings. Instead, she'd freeze him out as she had done after their kiss in the library. Had it not been for the incident with Lord Highcliff and the fact that she might have died but for his intervention, she would likely still not be speaking to him.

Still, there was much to admire about her aside from her face and her form. Her devotion to the children was obvious. The soothing presence she created in their lives and the sense of peace that always seemed to settle over them in her company was something to be envied. It was certainly a far cry from anything he had experienced in childhood—well, anything after his father's death.

Suddenly overcome with exhaustion, he removed his coat and waistcoat before tugging off his boots. Climbing into the bed, he flopped back against the pillows. Thoughts of his father prompted a wash of memories. He stared up into the ornate canopy with all its gilding and intricate drapery. In the center of it was a cherub-flanked medallion of a blue sky with fluffy white clouds.

Staring into that medallion, it seemed to shift before his eyes as he drifted into an uneasy sleep. It didn't take long for the dream to come. It always did when he was upset, or when he thought too much about his family before succumbing to sleep. It was the cold that invaded his awareness first, the bitterness of it. The sky above was leaden and heavy with snow clouds so thick that the whole world was cast in dimness. The only light came from the weak rays of sun filtering through that overcast sky. As they struck the snow-covered earth, they were amplified against the white backdrop until the glare was almost blinding.

He could recall his father's voice, the patient way he spoke, the gentle instruction in so many things. An ache spread throughout his chest because he knew what was to come. He wanted to shout a warning, to scream for them to run. But in the dream, he was locked into what he had done in that time, not what he would do given foreknowledge of those events.

Three dark shapes emerged from the trees, their faces indistinct, always blurred in his mind. He could hear the rough speech, the street cant. But he was unable to speak himself, unable to say anything as his father offered them generous hospitality. As a man observing it all in that dreamscape, he could now recognize the fear in his father's voice. He hadn't understood it as a child.

The next was all a blur, jumbled events that seemed to have no rhyme or reason, always in a different order. It was just the loud bang of a gun and his father falling. Someone shouting at him to run. His brothers falling to the ground.

The pain came then, sharp and splitting as it struck his forehead. Anytime he tried in his waking life to recall the events surrounding the deaths of his family, it was there, halting his progress, pulling him back to the present where he could escape it. But in the dream, for the first time, he didn't wake up in that moment. He wasn't given the option to avoid it. That time was different. That time, as he pushed past the pain, he dug into it, peering beyond the veil it had created over the rest of his memories. He could see his father lying in the snow, the red stain spreading outward from his body. And down the hill, he could see his brothers near the water's edge. He couldn't tell anything more than that they were both collapsed in the snow, unmoving.

But he could hear voices. In the distance, just at the edge of the tree line, they were talking—the three men who'd emerged from the woods and struck him before shooting his father and brothers. One looked back at him, guilt and remorse etched on his rough, craggy face. But it was the other man, the leader who turned in profile and shouted at him, that was who drew Barrett's gaze. He knew that face. He'd seen him that very morning.

Then the three of them disappeared into the trees, their voices growing slightly muffled. But there was another voice present. Cultured and smooth, upper class and achingly familiar. Try as he might, he could not put a name to it.

Barrett awoke with a start, his heart pounding and his breath coming in sharp, harsh pants. Sweat slicked his skin beneath his clothes, cold and clammy, as the linen of his shirt clung to his body. His muscles trembled with the strain of tension that gripped him. Everything was tight, so tight he feared moving even an inch would snap the muscles from the bones. It was all as terrifying as it was enlightening. But a part of him questioned it. Was he seeing only what he wanted to? Was the vision of that man at the scene of that horrid crime simply his mind's way of supporting his suspicions of Charlotte? He couldn't say. He didn't want to believe that, but he had to allow for the possibility.

Cursing, he climbed from the bed and rang the bell pull. Immediately, the man acting as his temporary valet appeared.

"A bath. As hot as you can make it," he ordered.

"Yes, your grace. Shall I have your evening clothes prepared?"

"Evening?"

"Yes, your grace. We are but two hours from dinner."

Barrett glanced at the clock on the mantel surprised to find that he'd slept for nearly four hours. But he was not refreshed from it. If anything, he was more haunted by his past than ever.

MINERVA HAD GIVEN Meredith lessons to complete on her own, simple things such as practicing her penmanship. That gave her an opportunity to work with John. Sitting down with him at a small table, she placed several objects on the table. "This is a ball, this is a bell, and this is a bonnet," she stated. "Do you know what all of these items are?"

He nodded.

She then took up a slate and wrote the letter "B" on it. "All of those words begin with a 'B'. That letter makes the 'buh' sound. You can make that sound, can't you?"

The boy nodded enthusiastically.

"All right, let's hear it," she said.

His face drew taut with concentration as he struggled to make his lips form the sound. Finally, after what seemed an interminable amount of time, he managed to stammer out the sound, "B—b—buh."

She smiled. "Very, very good. Now let's try an actual word, shall we? A simple one. Ball."

More stammering, a few false starts and finally he managed something that sounded like "baw".

"You are doing excellent work, John. Really! We shall have you speaking in no time at all."

For another half-hour they worked on that letter and all the associated words she could think of that would be simple enough for him to say. She wanted to build his confidence, after all, not send it smashing to the floor. In all, he did remarkably well. There was a slight stammer and he struggled to find words on his own, but he did quite well in just mimicking what was said to him.

"All right, that's enough for today," she said. "We will pick up again tomorrow and review all of this. Then we shall start on another letter... C perhaps."

The boy nodded eagerly, clearly excited by the prospect.

"You know, John used to speak," Meredith offered. "Not well, because he was only a baby. But I just remembered it. He would say lots of things and then one day he just stopped. And immediately afterward, Mama sent him away."

At the mention of their mother, John's face paled and his breathing became much sharper. He feared Mrs. Entwhistle-Graves, Minerva realized. Not wanting to lose the progress they had gained by getting him overset, Minerva nodded. "We will talk about that after dinner, Meredith... just the two of us."

Meredith glanced at her brother and saw his reaction. "Oh. Certainly, Miss Stone. After dinner then."

"John, some new clothes have been obtained for you. Aunt Sissy took care of that. Will you need help getting dressed?"

The little boy shrugged.

Minerva realized that he would have no notion of how clothes worked besides the rags he'd been given to wear in Bedlam—shirts that were overly large, breeches that tied with a bit of string to hold them on. The little breeches and waistcoat with a cravat would be impossible for the boy to navigate. "Put on the breeches and the shirt. I will help you with the rest. Meredith, your dress is fine since you changed after the park. Simply wash your face and hands and tidy your hair... I will return after I have changed my gown."

Leaving the children in the room that was serving as a make-shift schoolroom, she made her way down the corridor to her own chamber. Outside her door, she paused. What Meredith had revealed about John having been able to speak before was too significant a detail to keep from the duke. He would want to know that. And since speaking of their mother in front of the boy was not an option, it was best to do it now.

Turning away from her bedchamber, she moved further down the corridor to the more spacious and luxurious chamber that had been assigned to the duke. Knocking on his door, she heard a barked command to enter. So she did. Instantly, she regretted it.

He was seated before the fireplace in a large copper tub. Above the water line, she could see his broad shoulders, the firm muscles of his chest and the most fascinating swirls of dark hair that were matted to his flesh with water. She could not look away.

"Miss Stone... I thought you were one of the servants delivering more hot water."

"Umm... uhh... there was something of an urgent matter that I needed to discuss with you," she stammered. "But certainly, under the circumstances, I can wait until you have completed your... your... ablutions." Good heavens! She could barely form a coherent sentence.

"Clearly this has taken you by surprise," he said. "But I'm afraid you cannot leave just yet. If you do, you will surely be caught by the servants bringing water."

Even as he uttered the words, a soft knock sounded on the door. Minerva's eyes widened with panic. The duke looked at her and then pointed to a large chinoiserie screen, indicating that she should hide behind it. Unable to do anything else, she rushed past the tub and the very nude man who occupied it to duck behind that screen.

The temporary valet entered, two footmen following behind, and all of them carrying ewers of heated water. From the crack between the screen's panels, she could see them as they placed them near the edge of the tub.

"Your grace, shall I prepare to shave you before dinner?"

The duke shook his head. "No. If I elect to shave, I will see to it myself. In fact, I will also dress myself. You are dismissed for the evening. You may all go about your normal duties and tidy up in here while dinner is being served."

The servants all sketched their bows and backed out of the room. Minerva could not pull herself away from the small sliver of visibility between the panels. She watched with rapt attention as he lifted one of the ewers of water and poured it over himself, rinsing the last of the soap from his hair and his skin. Then he stood.

She didn't gasp. Somehow, she managed to hold that in. But dear sweet lord, he was perfection. Allowing her gaze to wander, much to her secret shame, she followed the lines of his long legs with their powerful and muscular thighs, up to the well-sculpted buttocks and the lean, corded strength of his back.

A part of her desperately wished for him to turn around, to solve some of the mysteries that remained in her mind about what he would look like beneath his clothing. But he did not, at least not immediately. He grasped one of the drying cloths from a nearby table and wrapped it about his waist, twisting the fabric to hold it in place.

"You may come out, Miss Stone."

Emerging from her hiding place, Meredith looked everywhere in the room but directly at him. "I did not mean to intrude, your grace."

"But you did intrude... Minerva. And given all that has been said and done, all that has transpired between us, I can only assume that you must have had a very good reason."

She did. And she was struggling to recall it. Finally, after a moment, she managed to pull the information to the forefront of her mind and share it. "Meredith recalled that John, as a young boy, could speak. He stopped speaking only a short time before his mother sent him to Bedlam. I wonder, if perhaps, he stopped speaking not because he was unable to do so but because he had been made to fear doing so? Even the merest mention of Mrs. Entwhistle-Graves seems to terrify him."

He nodded. "I cannot say, of course, but it seems plausible. Especially if he witnessed or overheard something that Charlotte would never want him to speak of... but Meredith is not the only one to be taken unawares by a forgotten memory."

"What does that mean precisely?" She was clearly puzzled by his revelation.

"In the past, I could recall certain events from the day my father and brothers were murdered. Going out with them to hunt... but from that point forward it is always a blank. I dream of it, and even in my dreams, I cannot see beyond that moment. Until today. I saw everything. It all came back to me through the course of that dream. I now know where I have seen the man who followed us earlier today... I believe, with all of my heart, that he was one of the men who committed such terrible violence against my father and brothers."

Minerva shook her head. "With every passing hour, this tale grows more and more twisted."

"It does," he agreed. "But now there is a more pressing question."

"And what is that?"

His gaze settled on hers, hot and hungry. "What did you see, Minerva?"

Her throat went dry. "I don't understand."

"Behind that screen, Minerva... what did you see?"

He closed the distance between them as she floundered for an answer. It wasn't until they were scant inches apart, until she could see the smallest bead of water trickling a delicate path over his skin, that he stopped. "I know you were looking," he said. "The question is, do you wish to see more? I will show you anything you desire. You have but to ask."

She could smell him. Clean skin, the linen wrapped about his waist, the scent of his soap—it was heady and intoxicating. It tempted her beyond measure. She wanted nothing more than to lean forward and taste his flesh, to lick those droplets of water from his heated skin. "I am a governess—"

"You are more than that. You happen to be a governess," he stated. He raised one hand to her cheek, stroking the skin there with his thumb in soft circles that made her want nothing more than to lean into him, to feel his strength and warmth flooding her. "You are beautiful, passionate, fiercely protective of children that you hardly know, gentle and easy with them in a way that most people cannot fathom. Intelligent, strong-minded, obstinate at times, with a quick temper and a siren smile. You are everything."

Breathlessly, she murmured, even as her eyes fluttered closed to savor his touch, "You should not say such things to me."

His hand halted its gentle caress. "Because you do not deserve to hear them... or because I do not deserve the honor of saying them?"

Her eyes flew open then and she stared at him in astonishment. "Because of situations... you are a duke... and I—there is no world in which we can escape the roles we have been born to."

"Damn the world. Damn our situation. And damn my title. I want you... I've spent my entire adult life denying myself everything as I struggled with the guilt and shame others heaped upon me. I am done with that. I want only to be happy. And nothing would make me happier than you."

The first gong sounded. They would need to be in the drawing room in only a quarter of an hour. It was a harsh intrusion of reality. "I must go," Minerva said, stepping back from him quickly.

"Then come back. Tonight. When the entire house is abed... come to me," he urged. "Think about it. Do not answer now. Just consider it."

Shaking, she nodded, and then quickly made her escape. Running to her chamber as if the very hounds of hell were at her heels, she closed the door behind her and leaned against it. Drawing in great, gulping breaths, she was more torn than she had ever been in her life. Everything she knew to be right was at war with everything she desired. And she had the duration of the evening meal to make a decision.

Chapter Twenty-Two

DINNER WAS TENSE. Minerva was terribly distracted and barely able to keep up with the polite conversation Sissy had initiated. The children were terribly well-behaved. John struggled with his utensils but Meredith was there to help him, to show him what to do. It was very sweet, in fact.

When dessert was finally served, her tension only increased. The meal was nearly at an end and she had yet to make up her mind. Would she go to him as he'd asked? As she, if she were entirely honest with herself, desired? Or would cowardice win again?

Lost in her own thoughts, consumed by her terrible quandary, she barely registered when a footman came to retrieve her plate. He took it away, her dessert nearly untouched.

"Was the trifle not to your liking, dear?" Sissy asked.

Minerva glanced up at her. "It was delicious, Sissy. With the events of the day, I'm afraid my appetite is not as it should be."

Sissy clucked her tongue sympathetically. "Of course. It was a very trying day! That awful man in the park... I cannot imagine what he was about. Dear heavens! I hesitate to think what might have occurred had Barrett not recognized what he was about and hastened to your side."

"You are quite right, of course," Minerva agreed. "We have much to be grateful for. Did I tell you that John is making excellent progress? He can say many, many words that I daresay he did not even know he was capable of." It was an obvious attempt to change the subject but no one protested.

Sissy turned to the boy and beamed. "Of course, he can. He's very intelligent! Anyone can see that! You will be talking up a storm in no time, John. With both Miss Stone and your very attentive sister to help you, there is nothing you are not capable of doing. Tell us what words you learned today."

"Sissy, you are embarrassing the boy," the duke interjected. "Leave him be to accomplish things because he desires to accomplish them. Not because he will be called out to demonstrate them like a trick pony."

John was looking at the duke then with something that could only be called adoration. No doubt, he saw the duke as quite heroic given that it was he who had liberated him from the institution and now spared him the anxiety of having to perform his newly learned vocabulary in front of others.

Then the duke favored the boy with a wink. It was a sly, playful gesture. Something she had never seen from him before, she thought. It warmed her heart, and it cleared away any lingering confusion for her. Whatever happened after the fact, she would go to his room. She would give herself to him. If his mistress was all she could ever be, then so be it. Wasn't it better to have a small piece of him than nothing at all?

"Well, let us all retire to the drawing room. Miss Stone, will you favor us with another of your enchanting pianoforte performances? Or am I embarrassing you, too?" Sissy asked with a sharp glance at Barrett.

"I'd be delighted," Minerva replied.

Upon entering the drawing room, she took up her position at the handsome instrument and launched into a passionate rendition of one of Beethoven's compositions. She'd chosen it because it was a piece she knew by heart and would require no thought from her at all, as she was clearly incapable of it at that moment. Her mind was entirely occupied with the decision she had made and what would come after the rest of the house was abed.

THE HOUSEHOLD HAD retired. Sissy had sought her chambers. Minerva had taken the children upstairs to tuck them into their beds. And he waited. Alone in his chamber, his valet dismissed, he simply waited. With no notion of what she had decided, he'd placed a bottle of brandy on a table near the fireplace. It was not the company he would choose, but it was the company he would console himself with if she elected to go to her virtuous bed alone.

Jerking at the knot in his cravat, he loosened the offending neckcloth before jettisoning it across the room. The damned thing was choking him half to death. He'd already stripped off his coat and waistcoat. He remained clad in his trousers and shirt along with highly polished boots. If he'd been the sort to care about such things, he would have to admit that his temporary valet was more than capable in his duties. It was a shame the man's talents were wasted on him.

The soft knock at his door halted any thoughts of the valet and his capabilities. It halted thought altogether beyond one. *She had come.*

Crossing to the door, he opened it wide and was greeted by the sight of Miss Minerva Stone still wearing one of the dark-hued gowns that Sissy had pushed upon her. It highlighted the alabaster nature of her skin and the soft silvery tones of her blonde hair. In the dimly lit corridor, her eyes were dark pools of uncertainty mixed with desire.

"I wasn't sure you'd come," he said.

"I wasn't either," she admitted.

He stepped back, ushering her inside, before closing and locking the door behind her. It shut out the world, insulating them in the dimness of his chamber so that it seemed they were the only two people in existence. It was terribly intimate, primarily because both of them understood, at least in the broad sense, why she was there.

She stepped into the room, pausing in the center of it, midway from the door to the bed. "I have no idea what I'm doing. Other than whispered conversations between girls at school when we were younger—and this sort of vague knowledge—the particulars of it are simply unknown to me."

He closed the distance between them, taking her hands in his. He placed one on his chest, directly over his pounding heart and pressed his hand over hers to hold it there. "There are particulars. There is what feels good, what feels right—there is an instinct about these things, Minerva, that will guide you. But you must be certain. If you have any doubts—"

"I have many doubts about many things… but not this. I want it, even if I'm not entirely certain what 'it' is." She took a deep breath, then looked up at him, meeting his gaze.

Rather than allow her nerves the time needed to get the better of her, he slid his hand down to her waist and tugged her against him. When their lips were just shy of touching, her lashes fluttered, her eyes closing as she sighed with a combination of need and relief. This, at least, would be familiar to her. Every seduction began with a kiss, after all.

Barrett observed her every response. After all, the kiss was the prelude to everything else. It would set the tone for the rest of it going forward. He allowed his hands to drift over her, lazily stroking her shoulders, her back, her arms, the curve of her waist and the flare of her hips. But it was, on the face of it, fairly benign and innocent. He had done nothing yet that she could not come back from. It was imperative to him that he not rush her, that she have ample opportunity to change her mind. How he prayed she would not! But it was the only honorable way to proceed, given that they had not yet made any promises to one another. He had expressed his intent to take a bride but he had not asked for her hand.

Until things were settled, until he had proven his innocence fully and proven Charlotte's guilt—to whatever degree she was involved—he did not feel that he was free to make such offers. He had never imagined that he would meet a woman in his lifetime who would tempt him to alter his stance on the matter. Always, he had been content to allow the title to descend to distant cousins. But the idea of Minerva having his children, of her body growing round and heavy with the child he planted within her, it was gratifying to him in ways that he could not explain. It was, after all, the most primal way a man could lay claim to a woman, to tie her to him forever.

She shivered against him, leaning closer, her fingers grasping his shirt with a kind of desperation that he understood only too well. It was the prompting he needed to shift direction, to take things to the next level. Taking his lips from hers, he trailed a burning path of kisses, nibbles and licks along the curve of her jaw to the shell of her ear, then down her neck to the gentle arc of her collarbone. A tremor of delight wracked her body.

Taking that as a sign of progress, Barrett walked her back to the bed, taking each step toward it like a dance. Only when the backs of her knees bumped the mattress did she open her eyes and gaze up at him.

"Do you make a habit of seducing young women, your grace?" she asked.

"No, Minerva, I do not… and I think, under the circumstances, it is certainly high time for you to call me by my given name… Barrett. Say it. I wish nothing more than to hear it on your lips."

"Barrett, then," she whispered. "You seem remarkably adept at calming the nerves of untutored young ladies."

He grinned. "Is that jealousy I hear from you, Minerva? Would it ease your mind to know that in my adult life, I have bedded only one woman. A single, long-time mistress. We parted ways last year as she received an offer of marriage from another gentleman. We were friends more than anything and I urged her to accept it as it would secure her future."

She blinked in surprise at that admission. "Really? I would have thought you... well, that is... you seem very experienced."

He grinned. "Then I am doing it right... or I was, until I let you distract me with your questions. Now, this will be much easier if we can divest you of some of these many layers of clothing."

"Oh," she replied pensively. "I suppose that would be all right then."

Carefully, he reached up and began freeing the buttons at the back of her gown, one by one. When the heavy fabric sagged from her shoulders, he gave it a tug so that it fell to her waist. It hung there on her hips for just a moment before falling into a puddle at their feet.

Clad in her stays, chemise and petticoat, he could see more of her than he ever had in the modestly cut clothing she preferred. Her breasts were more generous than he'd realized, rising bountifully above the gussets of her stays. With a single tug, he loosened the tapes of her petticoats and sent them slipping to the floor as well.

Sweeping one arm behind her knees and another behind her back, he lifted her and placed her gently on the bed. Pausing only long enough to remove his boots, he then climbed onto the bed with her, stretching out so that their bodies touched, chest to chest and hip to hip. It was maddening as it fulfilled one need— the desperate need to be close to her and to touch her—while stoking another to a fevered frenzy. It was so blatantly carnal that the urgency he felt to claim her, to bury himself in the tight, warm haven her body would provide had increased to the point of agony.

But she was not there yet. She was not ready for the things he would demand of her. It was his obligation to make her so.

He returned to her lips, kissing her with a renewed fervor even as his resumed their journey. This time, his exploration was not so innocent. He cupped her breasts, teasing the pebbled peaks until she was arching into his palm, straining for more. When she was moving desperately beneath him, only then did he tug the hem of her chemise upward, allowing his fingers to trail over the satin skin of her thighs.

When he stroked along her inner thigh, she tensed, but made no move to stop him. As his fingers brushed against the damp curls shielding her entrance, she made a whimper of sound—a sound of pleasure. Parting those soft folds, he slipped one finger inside her, finding the small, taut nub that would bring her the most pleasure. He stroked it gently at first, the lightest of caresses. Her eyes widened with wonder at the sensation. Then they fluttered closed once more as her hips arched upward from the bed in silent entreaty for more. And he gave it.

MINERVA HAD NEVER dreamed that her body was capable of such sensations, of such pleasure. She was searching for something, reaching for it, though she could not fathom what it was. But the feeling that something truly glorious awaited her had her pushing on, straining beneath him as she welcomed his touch eagerly.

When he lowered his head to her chest, his lips finding the pebbled peaks of her breasts even as his skilled fingers continued their journey between her trembling thighs, she was swept away by it. It was as if those areas of her body were somehow directly connected to one another, the sensations in one spot heightening and amplifying the sensations in another.

There was no embarrassment as he tugged the gussets of her stays down, freeing her breasts. It was only relief she felt that yet another layer between them had been stripped away. He teased her flesh. With lips, teeth and tongue, he drove her to this strange precipice, leaving her hovering there, waiting for something to happen.

"Not yet," he murmured against her skin. "Not just yet. I have more to show you, Minerva."

She had no idea what that "more" could be. If it was as shocking, as decadent and as life-altering as all that had gone before, she wasn't sure she'd survive it. But as he kissed his way down her ribs, over the softness of her belly, until he was nestled between her thighs, his face only inches from her most intimate areas, Minerva felt a moment of panic. "I don't know—"

"Trust me," he urged. "If you do not like it, you have but to say and I will stop."

It was a reasonable request. Despite the forbidden and taboo nature of what he was doing to her, she could not say no. With a nervous, jerky nod, she gave her tenuous consent.

The first brush of his lips was incredibly gentle, the softest hint of a kiss. It left her shivering in both anticipation and fear.

Then those caresses, while still gentle, became more insistent. She felt him parting her gently, his tongue sweeping inside her. All thought fled at that exquisite sensation. It robbed her of speech and reason. She could do nothing but let her head fall back on a pleasured moan as her hips arched upward to meet his questing mouth.

Shaking with it, her body wracked with tremors, she strained against him, climbing that familiar path to the precipice he'd pulled her back from only moments earlier. But this time, he did not stop. This time, he continued those gentle and insistent strokes until the tension that coiled inside her simply snapped. The wash of pleasure that exploded inside her was unlike anything she'd ever known. She cried his name softly, desperately, as the shuddering release left her weak—both replete and, at the same time, strangely unfulfilled—as if a beautiful thing had ended far too soon. Was there more? Surely, there was more. "You have not taken your own pleasure."

In response to her confused observation, he raised his head to meet her slightly befuddled gaze. "We are far from done, Minerva. That was only the beginning. A woman's body is a miraculous thing. Unlike a man who, once his pleasure has been taken, must recover before such amorous pursuits can be resumed, a woman is not so limited. You can achieve that pinnacle of pleasure over and over again. And I intend to see that you do."

Chapter Twenty-Three

"**M**A'AM, THERE IS a person here to see you," the aging butler said.

In her drawing room, the curtains drawn and only a single candle lit, Charlotte turned her head to glower at the man. "Who can possibly be here to see me? The house is shuttered and dark and we are reported far and wide to have vacated the city!"

"Forgive me, Madam, but it is not a social call. This... person... claims to be employed by you in a professional capacity. What the profession is one can hardly hazard to guess," the ancient retainer offered with a sneer of disapproval.

Pfife. It could be no one else. "I will see him in the study," she replied with a snap. Things had taken a turn now that Barrett knew of her youngest son's existence. He would no doubt have pieced together that she was behind it all. If he had not, it would only be a matter of time. Without an heir, she'd have had no reason to try and end his life—she'd only be trading one miserly duke for another. But with an heir at her disposal, one who would never be able to gainsay her, well, she'd only had to wait as long as she did to see his miserable life come to an abrupt end because at least one of her sons needed to have reached his majority. Willis was only months away from turning eighteen... just long enough to get everything sorted out and for him to seize control as his brother's guardian.

"Madam, forgive me, but this man does not appear to be of the trustworthy sort. I cannot imagine that being alone with him—"

"You are quite right. He is not trustworthy. One does not hire trustworthy people to do dastardly things! It rather defeats the purpose. Of course, had my sons not proved so utterly useless, it would not be necessary to hire anyone at all!" It would have been so much simpler had they simply managed to eliminate their cousin at Griffingate as they'd been initially directed to do. Barrett loved to go thundering across the fields at breakneck speeds, after all. Everyone locally said it was only a matter of time until he was found dead from a fall. It would have been the perfect solution. But no, someone, likely her brat of a daughter, had opened their mouth and let her little secret slip. Now they were struggling at the back end, trying desperately to recover from that setback.

As the butler shuffled out, Charlotte rose and followed a few paces behind him down the corridor to the door of the library. Stepping inside, she went immediately to the desk and retrieved the pistols from the top drawer, checking to ensure that one was properly primed and loaded. She returned the case to the drawer and concealed the one pistol she'd liberated in the folds of her skirts. She needed Mr. Pfife, but she was not so foolish as to trust him.

After a few moments, the butler entered, Mr. Pfife following behind him. The servant lingered until she sent him a withering glare prompting him to slink out like a scalded cat.

"You failed today," she stated.

"Depends on 'ow you look at it… I proved I could get close to 'im. I proved I could track him down wherever 'e is. Proved I could ferret out what's important to 'im so 'e'll make 'imself vulnerable. But I don't work for free. We did the job we were asked to all those years ago. This is a different job. It requires a different pay. You want 'im dead, you'll give me fifty pounds now, another fifty when it's done!"

That was more than she had in her possession. After all, her alibi was secured by claiming to be a guest of Dorinda Forsythe's near Bath. She could hardly claim that alibi if she was using her charge accounts in town. No, she'd been surviving like a commoner on a cash basis and it was a surprisingly difficult way to live.

"I will give you twice that once the job is done. But until the duke is dead, I have no access to those funds."

"You got things worth more than that," he said.

Charlotte shuddered in distaste.

The man laughed. "No bit of quim is worth fifty pounds. No... I meant sparklers. You got lots of fancy jewels, don't you now?"

"I'll offer them up as collateral. You may hold the jewelry until I can offer you cash."

"Do I look like a pawn broker?" he snapped, slapping one hand flat on the desk with enough force that the inkwell rattled and fell to the floor.

Nervously, Charlotte closed her hand tightly about the butt of the pistol. "Mr. Pfife, my jewels are renowned throughout the city. They've been talked about in multiple gossip sheets. If you were to show up to any sort of establishment that might purchase them from you, it would be an avenue for interested individuals to trace our acquaintance—that, sir, is something neither of us wants!"

He rose then, eyeing her suspiciously, "Fine. I'll keep them on hold. But if you think to play me... if you think to cut me out of my 'ard earned coin... I will come for you. And what I do to his grace will look like child's games compared to what I'll do to you. We clear?"

Charlotte nodded. "Certainly, Mr. Pfife. There is another matter now, and naturally, you will be compensated for the additional task. The little girl and the governess—they must die, as well. But the boy, the young boy is to come to no harm."

"She's your daughter, ain't she?" He asked the question as a man puzzled, but he didn't seem to be overly troubled by the notion of it.

"Right now, she is simply a complication. That is all. I cannot afford for her or that wretched governess of hers to get in my way. They both know just enough to jeopardize my plans... Meredith should die as quickly and painlessly as possible. The governess... well, she's an excellent opportunity for you to make a pretty penny, isn't she? Well-mannered girls like that fetch a fine price, do they not? Once your friends have finished with her, you may dispose of her as you like."

"I ain't no pimp."

Charlotte shrugged. "That is your prerogative, Mr. Pfife. I do not care, so long as she can no longer cause problems for me."

Pfife turned to walk away, but as he did, the toe of his dirty books struck the silver inkwell. He stooped to pick it up. Turning it over and over in his hand for a moment, he stuck it in the oversized pockets of his rough coat. "Call it a bonus." Then he walked out.

Quaking, Charlotte sank back in the chair. She needed him, but she wasn't so foolish as to not be terrified of him. The great lengths she was taking to ensure her future would only be worthwhile if she had a future.

The panel concealed in the bookshelves opened then and Peter rushed in, Willis right behind him. It was obvious that everything had been overheard.

"You're going to let him have her? You promised her to me!" Peter shouted.

"Well, I have to break that promise, Peter, for the good of us all. There will be other pretty governesses in your future whom you may molest at your whim," she offered, her exhaustion evident in her voice. "We'll need several for your idiot brother, after all."

"She's different!" he snapped.

Only because she'd bested him, only because he'd gotten too close to her one night, made his clumsy advances and been knocked on his arse for it, she thought bitterly. Peter and his ego, his obsession with women, would be the downfall of them all.

"Hush, Peter," Willis said. "Mother has proven just now that her loyalty to her children is not so great that she will not sacrifice us should we become inconvenient. Lest you find yourself at the less than tender mercies of Mr. Pfife like Meredith, I'd advise you leave it alone and seek your bed."

Charlotte looked past Peter to see the resolute expression on Willis' face. Of all her children, he was the most like her. He understood what the prize was. "Take your brother's advice, Peter. Do not test me. I am very tired now."

Willis moved toward the door, holding it open for his brother. Peter stepped through it, halted his footsteps, and then looked back at her. There was hatred in his gaze. It was only a moment, then he continued on leaving Willis behind.

Charlotte watched him go, knowing even as she did, that Peter would be a problem that only grew in proportion. He would have to be eliminated or he would destroy everything she'd worked for. With a nod at Willis, one of shared understanding, she watched him follow his brother from the room. When it was time, he would do what was necessary.

Chapter Twenty-Four

B ARRETT FELT THE tremors wracking her body, felt her coming apart beneath him once more. Only then, only when he'd brought her to the peak of pleasure for the second time, did he even consider taking his own. In the future—the future they would build together—there would be opportunity for the sort of hurried love making that couples well-known to one another could indulge in, when both parties were experienced enough to appreciate and to fully exploit one another's sensual weaknesses. But for this, for her first time, he wanted to give her so much pleasure, that the inevitable pain it would cause could be easily overshadowed.

"No more," she breathed weakly, a satisfied smile curving her lips. "What are you trying to do to me?"

Unable to resist the temptation, he dipped his head and nipped at the slender column of her neck eliciting a shiver from her. "Not even a little more?"

She placed one hand on either side of his face, forcing him to meet her gaze. "It cannot all be about me. Ignorant as I may be in practice, I am theoretically aware that you are supposed to receive some pleasure yourself."

"As much as I want this," he admitted, "and as much as I long to make love to you fully, I cannot promise that it will not hurt you. It is grossly unfair that women alone must bear that burden."

"Will the burden change if I bear it now or later?" she asked, her streak of practicality shining through even in that moment.

He couldn't halt the smile that tugged at his lips in response to that very governess-like question. "You are not my governess. I am not a recalcitrant child to be reasoned with."

She shook her head. "No. No you are not a child... and neither am I. My choice, Barrett, was made when I knocked upon your door. Make love to me. Make me yours."

No sweeter plea had ever been uttered. It would take a greater man than he could ever hope to be to deny her. Though it was wrong, though he had every intention to make her his wife as soon as he could, taking her innocence beforehand was a purely selfish urge on his part—a way to ensure that when he did ask, she would be obliged to agree. He understood that even if she did not. Honor—true honor—would have precluded that sort of behavior. But there was a selfishness in him, innate and irrefutable. So many things had been denied him in life, had been taken from him. He wanted to hold fast to her by any means necessary.

Moving between her parted thighs, he couldn't stop the sigh of pleasure when she opened more for him. That small gesture of welcome, that clear entreaty, stoked his desire for her to a fever pitch.

Parting her gently, easing his way in, he clenched his jaw tight and clung to what remained of his control, shredded though it was. The tight clutch of her body around him, the heat of her as he sank into her was beyond pleasure. It hovered somewhere on that fine line between intense pleasure and pain—the agony of wanting so much more after receiving a glimpse of paradise. And then she closed her eyes, her hands coasting delicately along his arms before sliding to his hips. Her fingers clutched at his flesh, urging him on, and he was helpless to resist.

Moving his hips, he withdrew just a bit before surging in again. Short, shallow thrusts to pique the tension and the need once more. When she was with him, when he knew that she was no longer simply basking in recent pleasure but actively seeking her release anew, only then did he plunge deep, taking her innocence and sheathing himself fully inside her in one sharp thrust. She didn't gasp in pain or cry out at the invasion. Instead, she went quiet and still for a moment. Taking that cue from her, he did so as well.

That moment gentled the harsh, glinting edges of his lust. It reminded him that he wasn't there simply to take and ease his own urgent needs. Beyond the physical, beyond the heat and the urges that would only be temporarily assuaged, there was something more profound in it all. More ephemeral and more terrifying for it. He wanted to care for her, to cherish and protect her. He'd long since decided that he would have her as his wife, but that moment showed him a small glimpse of what the reality of that would be. For a man so isolated, so alone for so very long, it was terrifying to think of any one person meaning so much to him. But the die was cast. Turning back was not an option for either of them. It eased the fear and the enormity of the situation. If there was one thing he'd learned in his life, inevitability would have its way and he could do nothing more than allow it to take him. They were, both of them together, tangled in some force of nature far greater than themselves. As with all things on that magnitude, all one could do was give oneself up to fate.

"I'm sorry," he whispered. "I'm sorry that I hurt you."

She shook her head. "I'm not. I'm not sorry about anything that's passed between us or anything that is yet to come."

Barrett dipped his head, taking her mouth in a gentle kiss as he surged deeply inside her. That kiss, that soft and sweet melding of their lips was his anchor, keeping him rooted in that gentle rhythm as he rocked inside, taking them both to that precipice of completion. Through it all, he watched her face. He catalogued every response, not just for future reference, but to savor it. It was the most perfect moment of his life. Far beyond pleasure, beyond the sensual wonder of it, he felt at peace. He felt perfectly, completely at home. As if for the first time in a very long time, he belonged somewhere. He belonged with her.

As her body trembled beneath him, the rhythmic spasms of her release triggered his own and he followed her over that razor's edge, down into the waves of pleasure that would surely drown them both.

THE ROOM HAD grown so quiet. Even their breathing had stilled. They rested there together in his bed, on the cusp of slumber, as the night settled around them. Despite the silence, it was comfortable. There was no need to fill it up with words.

Her own feelings were impossible to define—impossible to put into words. She was much too practical a creature to ever think they had fallen in love so quickly. Love, to her way of thinking, was much more than the first rush of infatuation or desire. It was those things, but mingled with friendship, with trust, with shared experience... and with a choice. The choice of fidelity and constancy.

What lay between them was the promise of what might be, not what currently was. And she would not sully what had been a shockingly beautiful if impossibly carnal experience by thinking that it could ultimately lead them to nowhere. Such thoughts were shadows meant to be explored another day. Any other day.

"You are thinking very loudly," he murmured.

"There is no volume to one's thoughts," she argued.

He laughed softly, the sound fluttering her hair. "Then you have been left alone with yours for very long. There is indeed. But it is your body that gives you away. The tension is seeping in again... and I would swear an oath that I have done all in my power and beyond to leave you a boneless heap of decadent and well-pleasured femininity."

Minerva started to protest, but it died on her lips. Such a protest would be a lie. He was perfectly right and perfectly astute in his observations and his claims. "So you have. It would be ungracious of me to spoil your efforts."

He turned onto his side so that his body cradled hers entirely. It was the most natural thing in the world to follow suit, to sink back against him and feel herself surrounded by his strength and warmth. When his arms closed about her, pulling her in tighter, she relished that feeling of sanctuary—of being possessed by him.

Tomorrow, she thought. Tomorrow would come soon enough and bring its problems with it.

Chapter Twenty-Five

"**I** REALLY LIKE her," Meredith said. It was possibly the hundredth time such a declaration had been uttered as the little girl gazed adoringly at the doll her cousin had provided her.

Minerva bit back a smile as she patiently waited for John to sound out the word in front of him. They had worked on letters that morning and the sounds they made. That afternoon, they were forging ahead into combining them to form very simple words. It was a nontraditional method, to teach speech, spelling, handwriting, and reading all at once, but under the circumstances, she felt compelled to do so. He was lacking in so many areas. If she could help him to see progress in even one, it would build his confidence so. After all, he didn't know it was an unorthodox approach and he seemed to be grasping quite a bit of it.

When John had finished, Minerva replied to Meredith. "I'm certain he will appreciate that sentiment very much. When we join everyone for dinner, you must tell him how thoughtful his gift was and thank him for it. And when we're done with this, John, we will work on saying thank you if you would like."

The boy nodded.

"Try to say it... say yes," Minerva instructed. "It's a tricky word, but practice will make perfect."

The boy produced an approximation of the word. It came out more as "thes" but she would take the effort and call it a victory.

She smiled at him. "That was very good, John. You have come leaps and bounds in the few days you have been here. In no time at all, you will be saying whatever you please."

He smiled shyly, clearly pleased with the praise. But it was the way he leaned into her side, nuzzling his head against her, that truly melted her heart. Minerva wanted to scoop both of those children into her arms and hold them tight forever. Forgotten, she thought, but then realized that forgotten means they would have to have first been recognized. Their mother had never cared for them, not in the way a mother should. To her, they'd been pawns to be used in her schemes. It was beyond maddening.

"Are you all right, Miss Stone?"

Minerva looked up to see Meredith watching her warily. "I'm just fine, Meredith. I was only thinking very hard about something that was mildly unpleasant and not at all worth the upset it caused. Thank you for interrupting such a ridiculous waste of a perfectly fine afternoon. In fact, it is so fine outside that I suggest leaving off with studies altogether! We cannot go to the park, but there is an excellent tree for climbing in the back garden and I think that John should like very much for you to show him how to do so!"

Meredith twirled her doll around in a fair approximation of a country dance as she whooped with joy.

"Now, now... there is no need to leave off with decorum entirely," Minerva reminded her. "Get your coat on then help your brother with his. I shall put on my pelisse and gloves and meet you back here shortly."

Easing out into the corridor, leaving the children to don their warmer things, all recently delivered by various tradesmen and all of it taken easily in hand by Aunt Sissy who had made herself rather scarce of late, Minerva reflected on that. She knew, of course, what Sissy was about. She was letting them play house, so to speak. She wanted to give them the illusion of being a family together so that they might actually become one. It was an impossibility but she intended to savor this little kernel of time for all that it was worth. The real question remained of what she would do when it came to an end. Did she have the strength to remain for the children she loved so dearly even when the man she feared owned a piece of her soul would never be truly hers?

Moving down the corridor toward her own chamber, she had just reached her door when it opened and a hand closed over her wrist to yank her inside. There was no time to scream as a pair of strong arms closed around her and her lips were covered in a crushing kiss. Then the urge to scream faded entirely as she gave herself up to that achingly familiar kiss.

It was quick, filled with affection and heat, but over far too soon. When he pulled back from her, Barrett was smiling down at her. "I've been waiting in here for what feels like ages."

"You should not be lurking in my room," she admonished as she disentangled herself from his embrace and moved to the wardrobe to retrieve her pelisse. "What if I had taken you for a housebreaker?"

"You'd have struggled valiantly and somehow we would have found ourselves on the bed—"

"You're incorrigible," she retorted, but the censure was tempered by barely restrained laughter. "I'm taking the children into the garden to climb trees. They need to be outside while the weather is still warm enough to do so. I fear we will have snow before the week's end."

His smile faded. "I hate the snow."

There was something in his tone, something dark that caused her to glance back at him with concern. "Because of your family? What happened to them?"

The brief nod that was his response was all that he intended to offer. She could tell from the set of his shoulders. Draping her pelisse over the bench at the foot of the bed, she went to him, rubbing his shoulders gently. It was a touch intended to comfort and he accepted it as such, leaning into it and into her.

"You could come outside with us," she offered. "The children would certainly enjoy seeing you at play. No doubt you would do far better at teaching them to climb trees than I would."

He laughed softly, though the sound was a bit forced. "I would enjoy seeing you climb a tree to be sure. But no. The solicitor will be here shortly. I need to take the necessary steps to see that John's future and his freedom are secured and that Charlotte cannot simply reclaim the children at whatever juncture she chooses. I will not have them going back to her... not for any reason."

The relief she felt at hearing those words was beyond measure. She'd known he would not, of course, but that he was being proactive and taking such measures now eased her worries significantly. "Very well. Then they shall simply have to suffer through my substandard instruction in this area... and I will see you for tea this afternoon."

"And at dinner?" he asked with a hint of suggestion.

"And after dinner in the drawing room," she replied teasingly.

"And after the drawing room, in my chamber?" There was no suggestion or teasing in that. It was only a promise of mind-numbing pleasure.

"There's nothing I want more," she admitted. "But for now, you have to go. And you have to do it discreetly."

"Are you worried for your reputation?"

"Yes," she replied. "As should you be. I will not lose the children's respect because the household believes me to be a trollop!"

"And if they thought you were a future duchess?" he asked.

Minerva's heart stilled. Normally it pounded in his presence as though she'd run a race, but in that moment, nothing. When it began anew, it was erratic, making her feel dizzy and faint. "You can't be serious."

"I most certainly can. I wasn't going to say anything... not yet. But I don't want to wait. I don't want to spend another day without you knowing what you mean to me. No other woman will ever make me feel as you do, Minerva. I want you to be my wife."

She shook her head. "No. No, I won't do that to you. You must marry someone who can help you! Your position in society has been so precarious for so long, Barrett, that if you marry someone so low it will never improve things for you—"

"Then I will never marry," he said. "And society can hang. You are the only woman, Minerva. The only woman. It will be you or no one. Could you honestly, after what has passed between us, ever marry another man?"

"I never planned to marry at all," she admitted. "But no. I could not. I would not. But I cannot give you an answer now... I cannot think. I never expected this."

"You expected that I would dishonor you? That I would take your innocence with no thought to what was right and moral? Do you truly think so little of me?" It was clear from his tone that he was gravely insulted by that thought.

"Not at all. I had anticipated, honestly, that you would ask at some point. I just had not been prepared in this moment to hear it... but you must know what my answer was always going to be. I am not for you, Barrett. I am not meant to be a duchess," she admitted sadly.

"We are meant for each other. Were I a pauper, a prince or a goddamned pirate... we were meant for each other!" he snapped. "Your snobbery will not change that."

"Snobbery?" Minerva gaped at him. "I am not a snob. How dare you accuse me of that? I am a realist and I am trying to spare you the censure of your peers."

"They are not my peers. They have not been my peers since my father bled to death in the snow three yards from me. I will never be accepted by them, Minerva. Regardless of whom I marry, regardless of any degree of contrition I might show them—nothing will change their minds about who and what I am. So why in the name of all that is holy should I let them dictate any course in my life?"

She had no response for that. Silence stretched between them for a long moment, then he simply turned on his heel, marched toward the door and exited. Alone, she exhaled sharply as she fought back futile tears. When she had her emotions in hand, she donned her pelisse and went to meet the children. But she was distracted all the while by the wistful thoughts of what she might have if only she could be brave enough to reach out and take hold of it.

PFIFE PERCHED ATOP the garden wall. Hidden behind a large corbel on one side and the thick branches of a tree on the other, he was fairly certain no one would see him. The uppity bitch had given her orders but she had no idea what sort of undertaking she was asking of him. Committing three murders in the heart of Mayfair without getting caught would be a stretch for anyone. The house was full of servants. They'd be on him the moment one of them screamed. So the answer had been an obvious one. Get them out of Mayfair. For that, he needed leverage. The smallest and weakest would be the trick. If he could get his hands on one of the children, the duke and the governess would follow.

The terrace doors opened and a warmly clad trio emerged from the house. Just as he'd suspected, the pretty governess had brought the children outside for some air. With the park no doubt off limits now, the back garden had been her only option.

Carefully easing his weight down from the top of the stone fence, he crouched behind the bushes there and waited. The little boy was very quiet, the small girl more animated. The governess seemed to be somewhat subdued. A tiff with her lover, the duke, no doubt. It was an advantage. She'd be distracted by her own thoughts.

"Have you ever climbed a tree before, Meredith?" the governess asked.

"No, Miss Stone. Mother never permitted it when we were anywhere else. And there were no trees in our terrace at home, as you know."

"Right," the governess answered. "Then I will climb up a bit first and show you how it's done, all right?"

"Is it considered unladylike to climb trees?" the little girl asked.

"Very much so," the governess answered with a quick grin. "So I know you shall enjoy it thoroughly."

Pfife bided his time. He wasn't above enjoying the view a bit as the governess hiked her skirts to her knees and climbed up into the lower branches of the tree. He waited, carefully gauging that she was too high to simply jump down without injuring herself, before he made his move. Lunging out of the bushes, he grabbed the child closest to him—the girl and made for the gate.

The governess was shouting, screaming for him to stop even as she jumped from the tree to pursue them. The little boy stood silently by as he raced toward the garden gate with the crying child draped over his shoulder. Once on the other side of the gate, he tossed her into the empty sack in the back of the cart as it shot forward, his well-paid accomplice taking off quickly.

Inside the sack, the girl was screaming still, wailing loudly and kicking as violently as she could. Reaching down, he found the rounded lump that was her head and gave it a slight whack. "'Shush your squalling or I'll give you sum'in to squall about."

They hadn't even made the end of the mews, delayed by other carts and ambling servants, before the governess caught up to them. Her normally tidy hair was trailing behind her, the pins having been lost in the chase. It was, to his mind, a stroke of luck. With both of them in his hands, the duke would have to come for them. He'd never let them both go. Not the way that woman looked.

"Stop the cart," he told his accomplice sharply.

When the cart slowed, the governess reached them quickly enough. She was grabbing at the sack with the girl tied up in it even as he was grasping her arms and hauling her up into the back with them. She fought like a tigress. So much so that others were beginning to look their way. Drawing that much attention was too much of a risk. So he picked up a brick from the bed of the cart and smacked her on the head with it. Instantly, she went quiet and still. A trickle of blood muddied the golden strands of her hair just above her ear. It would be a pity if he'd killed her so soon. But it was what it was either way.

"Drive on... and make it quick. We need to be away from this place," he said.

Then the cart maneuvered out onto the main thoroughfares of Mayfair, disappearing into a sea of similar vehicles making their daily deliveries of goods to those that could afford them.

Chapter Twenty-Six

B ARRETT WAS IN the library. The solicitor had gone. All the necessary forms had been signed so that Charlotte would have the fight of her life in store if she meant to remove either Meredith or John from his care. It was the one thing that had gone well that day, he thought.

He'd bungled things with Minerva. He had thought better of rushing her with talk of the future, but then he'd gone ahead with it regardless and now things were—difficult. Ultimately, it changed nothing except the timeline. His intentions would not be altered and his resolve would not shift. He needed her to understand where his heart lay. It might take her longer to come round to it, but it had to happen.

A knock at the door drew his attention away from his own brooding thoughts. "Come," he called out, anticipating that it would be the butler with some sort of correspondence or nuisance of a caller. But it was Sissy who stood there hesitantly in the doorway clutching John's hand as the boy wailed hysterically.

"What on earth has happened?" Barrett asked.

"I found him in the garden," Sissy said. "I went to the morning room to retrieve my needlework and I just heard him crying so piteously. But he was alone outside, Barrett. I cannot fathom that Miss Stone would have let him wander off alone."

Barrett's heart dropped to his stomach, settling there like a brick. "No, she would not have." Getting to his feet, he walked over to the boy and knelt in front of him. "John, I'm not angry with you, but you must stop crying. I have to ask you what you saw."

The little boy continued to sob, but he nodded dutifully as he swiped ineffectually at his tears with the back of his hand.

"Were Miss Stone and Meredith in the garden with you?"

A nod, accompanied by louder wailing.

"Did they leave of their own accord?"

This time, the boy shook his head.

Barrett's blood was rushing in his head, the sound of it drowning out everything else. The acrid and bitter taste of fear was rising up in his throat, filling his mouth as he forced out the next question. "John, did the man who was in the park yesterday take them?"

And then John wailed even louder, his little face red and his cheeks soaked with tears. The boy simply cried as if his entire world had ended.

Reaching out, Barrett cupped the little boy's damp cheeks. "Do not worry. I will bring them both home. Whatever it takes, I promise you, I will bring them home… and nothing will separate us again. Do you believe me?"

The boy nodded, clinging to Sissy's hand with one of his and clutching Barrett's shoulder with the other. Still, he nodded with all the faith his little body could muster.

It was an impulse more than anything, but Barrett leaned forward and kissed the top of the child's head. "Stay here with Sissy. Do as she says and be a very good boy. I will have them home as soon as I can."

"Where are you going?" Sissy demanded.

"To beard the lioness in her den," he said. "All this started with Charlotte. It will bloody well end with her."

Sissy let out a sigh that was both relief and fear. "Oh, please do not underestimate her. We both know her to be a cunning foe."

Barrett was already back at his desk, prepping the same pistols he'd taken with him the day before. Satisfied that everything was as it should be, he met her worried gaze. "There is too much at stake. I will not underestimate her, Sissy, but make no mistake... she had best not underestimate me. I will see all of this at an end one way or another," he vowed. "Take John, get him something to calm him, put him to bed. I will not return here without them."

Not a single one of them offered up the one terrible thought which plagued them all. He may not have a choice.

HER HEAD WAS aching beyond measure. Her back was not much better for it. Opening her eyes slowly against even the dim light which filtered into the foul-smelling space where she currently rested, she struggled to make sense of it all.

Instantly, she registered two things. The first, she was not alone in that space. Meredith lay curled on the floor beside her, hands and feet bound with a gag tied about her mouth. As she was trussed herself and not gagged, she could only assume the child had been peppering their captors with questions or demands. The second thing she realized was that they were in very dire straits, indeed. She had no notion of where they were and her knowledge of the city of London was fairly limited. Beyond the streets of Mayfair and popular shopping districts, she had no notion of how to navigate it. Even if they could manage to escape that hovel-like room, she might well lead them to a far worse fate than the one which currently awaited them.

Propping her bound hands on the floor behind her, Minerva managed to push herself to a sitting position. There was a post behind her and she leaned against it until the first wave of dizziness and nausea passed. Moving her head gingerly, she beckoned Meredith closer. The child half-scooted, half-hopped over to her. Leaning down, using her chin and shoulder, Minerva managed to dislodge the cloth tied around the girl's face that held her gag in place. Immediately, however, she made a shushing sound.

"We must be quiet," she urged in a low whisper. "We do not need to give them cause to separate us or to think we might be up to anything. I need you to listen carefully and when you respond, you must whisper. All right?"

Meredith nodded. "You've been asleep ever so long. I thought you had died."

"Things are not so dire just yet," Minerva replied, smiling in spite of everything. "Do you know where they've brought us?"

"No. But it smells horribly of fish outside and through gaps in the building when they brought us in, I could see tall ships on the other side."

They were at the docks. Not an area she was too familiar with, but it was at least a starting point. If they could keep the river behind them and if St. Paul's was visible in the distance, she might manage to get them home. Whether or not she could find her way to the house they were staying in with Sissy was certainly questionable, but the Darrow School... that she was at least reasonably certain of.

"Scoot around behind me, with your back to me, and I will try to untie your hands," Minerva instructed her. "But be quiet. Above all things, be as quiet as you can. And if someone comes in, do not argue and do not ask questions. We have no notion what sort of people we are dealing with and making them angry could go very badly for us."

When Meredith was in position, Minerva began to feel about, checking the sort of knots that had been used. She was hardly the expert, but one of the other students at the school, years ago, had spent an inordinate amount of time with Navy men. She'd taught them all she could about the knots they'd shown her.

It was no mean feat. After multiple failed attempts, her fingertips were raw from the rough texture of the rope and she'd managed to pick up multiple splinters from the wooden floor and the heavy beam she rested against. Still, after many long and stressful minutes, the ropes at Meredith's wrists went slack.

Immediately, she felt Meredith tugging at the ropes that held her wrists fast. Clumsier in her efforts, the child was both relentless and enthusiastic. Eventually, the knots gave under her multiple attempts and the pins of needles of all the blood rushing back to her fingertips had Minerva biting her lip to hold back a groan of pain.

When she felt she could move her fingers with some degree of grace, she leaned forward to tackle the bonds at her ankles. A noise outside the door made her stop immediately. Tucking her freed hands behind her back, she whispered at Meredith to restore her gag and hide her hands. The child had just finished when the heavy door was unlocked and the man stepped inside— the same man who had been after them in the park.

He was larger than she recalled, filling up the doorway with his raw-boned frame. There was an air of menace about him that was far more pronounced in that dank, dirty little room with no witnesses and no one else to protect them. She wasn't so refined and so delicate that she could not defend herself if she needed to, but she was also not foolish enough to think they wouldn't be far better off if it didn't come to it. After all, she'd have the element of surprise on her side only one time and if she squandered it, she'd pay for it with her life.

"Quiet as little mice," he mused with a grin, eyeing them coldly, like a cat with the aforementioned prey.

"What do you want?" Minerva demanded. "We've done nothing to you."

"No. Not to me. I couldn't care less one way or another whether the two of you lived or died. But you've made it 'ard for someone else, 'aven't you? Now, she wants you all gone. And I've got to figure out if it serves me better to please 'er, or to see if the duke thinks you're worth trading for."

"Trading what?" Minerva queried.

"My freedom, my life… and the truth about what 'appened to 'is family," the man said. "So just keep being quiet. Don't make me angry. Don't make a fuss. You might get out of it all yet. Then again, maybe not."

He stepped out once more, leaving them alone. But Minerva was not so foolish as to take him at his word. She could see the shadows of his feet beneath the gap at the bottom of the door. He was waiting for them to say something, to do something that would make his decision for him. But at their continued silence, he finally moved off, his heavy footfalls carrying him down the corridor.

"Should we wait, then?" Meredith asked, having finally given up all pretense and removed her gag once more.

"Not if we can help it. It's all about opportunity, however," Minerva replied. "We cannot simply run out the front door. We need to see if there is another way out of this room, out of this building, whatever it is, that will allow us to get away unseen."

"There is a window," Meredith said, pointing up to where the dim light filtered in through.

Glancing at it, Minerva didn't dismiss it out of hand. It was very high, but there were crates and other things littered about the room that, so long as they moved quietly, they might be able to climb upon to reach it.

Getting carefully to her feet, Minerva took each step with extreme caution. She tested each floorboard for a whisper of a creak before resting her weight on it fully. Meredith was following behind her, treading only where she did until they reached that window. There was a crate already placed beneath it and Minerva had to wonder about its placement. Had some other unlucky soul also been considering escape from their current prison? There was a scrap of lace on the floor next to it, torn from the hem of a dress. It made that seem a likely scenario. What disastrous fate had waited for that poor girl?

Realizing that such thoughts would only dishearten her and hinder their escape, Minerva forced them aside as she climbed gingerly onto the crate and peered out. Carefully, she opened the window, daring not to make a sound. Rising on her toes, she peered over the edge of the sash and could see a small ledge that, if they were lucky and fortune smiled on them, they might be able to stand upon to make their way to the next building over. Its roof sloped down further still toward the ground.

"I think we can do this," she said to Meredith with far greater confidence than she actually felt. "But I'm going to help you out first. Do you know what St. Paul's looks like? The big domed-roof church?"

"Yes, of course, I do. You showed it to me whenever we walked anywhere," Meredith replied with no small amount of impatience.

"Right. And, of course, you were always paying attention. Once we are out of here, if we get separated, you must follow the sight line of St. Paul's. Once you are in a better part of the city, you must simply ask for help to reach the Darrow School. Can you remember all of that?"

"Yes. I will remember it all, but we will not be separated," the little girl stated resolutely. "That simply must not happen."

"I hope it will not… and, Meredith, I've no wish to speak ill of your mother, but if you should happen to encounter either her or your brothers, run the other way. I cannot explain more, but there is something foul afoot and I very much fear that they may all be in the center of it," Minerva warned sternly.

The little girl had no flippant response to that. Her chin quivered a bit, but then she stiffened it and gave a jerky nod. "I understand."

Stepping down from the crate, Minerva helped Meredith onto it and then through the open window. Climbing up once more atop it herself, she lowered the little girl until her booted feet were on the ledge and then guided her over so that she herself would have room to climb out.

The task was not as easy as it had initially appeared, especially in skirts that snagged on every bit of loose wood or protruding nail. Finally, with her feet on the ledge, her skirts swishing around her legs from the breeze off the river, they began to make their way over to the next building. In the reality of the moment, it felt and looked much higher than it had when they'd had their feet planted on the floor inside that dingy room. Still, at least outside, there was a chance at escape. Inside, they had simply been awaiting what would likely have been a brutal fate. She would not allow her fear to prevent them from taking any opportunity that presented itself for them to save themselves.

They'd just reached the corner of the building, Meredith jumping down gamely onto the slightly lower roof of the neighboring structure, when she heard the shouting behind her. A glance over her shoulder and she saw the large man who'd taken them peering out at her with murder in his eyes.

They were out of time.

Chapter Twenty-Seven

"WHERE IS SHE?" Barrett demanded as he stormed into the still-smoky structure of the family's Mayfair home.

"Your grace, Mrs. Entwhistle-Graves, as I've said, is in Bath—"

Barrett didn't let the man finish. "She'll be swinging at Tyburn before I'm done with her. You will tell me where she is and where her other miscreant children are, or regardless of your age, I will beat it out of you!"

"Your grace!" the man squawked in alarm, moving away from him so quickly he bumped into a table with his retreating form and nearly dislodged what appeared to be a poor copy of an expensive vase that had once rested there.

"Tell me! I will have the truth from her once and for all!"

"Mother isn't here."

Barrett turned to the sound of that voice, spotting Willis standing in the doorway to the drawing room. "What are you doing here? Why are you not still at Griffingate?"

"Did you honestly think it was just a series of misfortunes that befell you on the way here from Yorkshire?" Willis demanded. "That was me and Peter acting upon Mother's orders. She'd wanted you to simply have an accident while out riding, something that would see you dead finally. But then Meredith and that blasted governess had to open their mouths and ruin everything by telling you of John's existence. With you hying off to London, we had no option but to follow and try to eliminate you along the road."

"Such an admission could see you hanged," Barrett pointed out.

"I'm aware. But I'm also aware that you do not want to court further scandal... and I'm prepared to provide the information you require in exchange for my future. I want a commission in the army. A good one that will allow me to make a decent living for myself far from Mother, if she escapes this all unscathed, and far from Peter who will likely get himself killed if left to his own devices."

It was the first admission of any sort from any of them. Barrett would take what he could get. "Consider it done."

"Mother met with a man named Mr. Pfife here the other night. They've apparently met before at a wharf-side tavern called The Goose and Garters. He conducts his business from there."

"And where is she now? Your mother?"

"She and Peter left earlier... she means to see him dead eventually because he will not be swayed from his obsession with Miss Stone," Willis admitted. "And she means to see Meredith dead, as well, because unlike Peter and me, Meredith seems to have been the only child born to her that is neither an imbecile nor an unconscionable monster."

Barrett said nothing about those assertions. Peter was a monster. Willis was very close to becoming one. But John was hardly an imbecile. Still, he had what he needed. "You'll get your commission. If your mother returns here, and your brother, do whatever is necessary to keep them here until I can return. I will see this situation remedied one way or another."

"You were not supposed to survive... the day your father and brothers were killed," Willis continued. "Mr. Pfife was one of the killers Mother and your uncle engaged to see an end to the lot of you. She'd intended to make herself a duchess even then, you see?"

"I know. I've been piecing it all together over the last day or so. Seeing his face brought it all back... if your mother had left well enough alone, she likely would have become a duchess before the end of it all anyway."

"Patience was never her virtue. Save Meredith if you can. And save Miss Stone from Peter. Heaven knows what he would do to her if given his way," Willis replied. "I'm not like them. I am not overly troubled by a conscience but I do not actively enjoy hurting people."

Barrett said nothing in return. Willis simply retreated once more into the drawing room in silence. Turning back to the butler, Barrett pointed at him directly. "If you breathe a word of warning to your mistress, you will swing beside her."

"Yes, your grace," the chastened man murmured before shuffling as quickly down the hall as he could.

With no time to waste, Barrett left the house once more, closing the door on that hellish space for what he hoped would be the last time. He would sell it and all the painful memories it held for everyone who had ever lived within its walls. Or let it burn. Either way, he didn't care.

Hailing a hack, he gave the driver the address. If the man thought it odd to be taking a gentleman from Mayfair to such a location, he wisely kept his questions to himself.

SCRAMBLING OVER THE edge of the sloping roof to a dirty alleyway below, Minerva scraped her leg on a broken board. There was no time to assess the damage or treat the injury, so she simply grasped Meredith's hand and took off, running past back entrances to various buildings. She could hear the man in pursuit behind them, but she didn't look back. Forward. Forward was the only direction they could afford to look.

A smallish opening appeared ahead of them, cutting between two buildings. It was narrow enough that their pursuer would have to turn sideways to get through, making it perfect for them. Ducking into that space, pulling Meredith behind her, she dodged rats, refuse and all manner of unspeakable things as they raced ahead, desperate to avoid recapture.

When they emerged, there was a proliferation of untidy and derelict establishments lining the streets. There was also a very familiar carriage—Mrs. Entwhistle-Graves was far from her natural habitat.

With Meredith's hand clasped in hers, Minerva went to the left and then immediately moved into a crouch behind a stack of barrels and crates at the corner of a building. They would be entirely concealed from view. But she had no doubt that once their abductor emerged from the alley, he would be far more interested in speaking with the woman she suspected to be his employer than giving chase to them.

Seconds later, when the man stepped onto the sidewalk mere inches from where they were hiding, she knew she'd been right. She heard the vile curse words pouring from his mouth as he talked about an "uppity bitch". Then he was crossing the street, heading for a dilapidated tavern called The Goose and Garters. Committing that name and everything else she could to memory, she gathered Meredith close. Once it was clear, they sped off on foot. If they could get close enough to hail a hack, she'd see them to the Darrow School that way, concealed and safely tucked inside. Effie would pay the cost on their arrival.

One street over, they found their chariot. The aging hack with its very sad-looking horse would never do in the better parts of town. But there, on those streets, it blended in.

"Can you get us to the Darrow School in Mayfair?" she asked the driver. He was wearing a worn coat and oddly dapper hat.

"I can. Can you pay?"

"You will be paid on our arrival. Miss Darrow herself will see to it," Minerva stated. "I beg of you, sir. We have been abducted and brought here against our will. We must return home at once to assure others of our safety or the outcome could be quite terrible. Please?"

The driver scanned them with an appraising eye, taking in the cut and fabric of their clothing, their manners. When, at last, he appeared satisfied, he said, "Up you go. Up and in. I'll likely regret it, but can't have two babes in the woods like the lot of you running around here! More nabobs in Spitalfields than in Mayfair today!"

Uttering a silent prayer of thanks for the man's kind nature despite their current surroundings, Minerva helped Meredith hoist herself into the carriage and then quickly followed suit. But as she began to follow suit, the driver's words gave her pause.

"What other nabobs? Did you perchance bring a gentleman to this tavern?" She demanded.

"Aye. Handsome fellow. Rougher-dressed than most gentlemen would be," the driver explained.

Minerva glanced at the tavern and then back at Meredith's worried face. "Take this child to the Darrow School. Miss Darrow will pay you for your trouble... Meredith, your cousin is in there with your mother and with that man who took us. He may need my help."

"I'm scared!" the little girl said. "I don't want to go alone."

"I don't want you to, either, but sometimes we must be very brave even when we are terribly frightened. You get to the school. Mrs. Wheaton and Miss Darrow will look after you until Barrett and I can come for you. You must be brave for now. Please?"

The little girl nodded tearfully. "Be careful. Please. I don't want it to be like before. I don't want to live with Mama and Peter. I want to stay with you and Cousin Barrett!"

"And that is precisely what you shall do," Minerva promised, though she realized it was not entirely in her power to provide. So many things were still up to chance. "But for now, we cannot do what we need to do until we know you are safe. We will come for you as soon as we can!"

Closing the door to the hackney and banging on the side of it to send the driver on the way, Minerva watched it disappear into the traffic. It hurt her to send Meredith off alone, to know the child was frightened but her hands were tied. Barrett was in that tavern and was outnumbered at present. She had to do what she could to save him—to save them all.

Chapter Twenty-Eight

INSIDE THE DIM interior of the tavern, Barrett was not alone. He'd made a strategic stop on his journey to The Goose and Garters at the home office of the Bow Street Runners. It was a little known fact that for years he'd been paying a few officers in their ranks to continue investigating his father's murder. Those gentlemen were even now lurking within the confines of the tavern, waiting for something to occur. What particularly that might be was anyone's guess—that is until his aunt walked into the establishment.

The pelisse and oversize bonnet she wore did little to disguise Charlotte. Though he suspected that she was not interested in hiding at the moment. She rather thought she'd won, he surmised. Charlotte believed that in taking Minerva and Meredith, she'd have left him vulnerable to whatever she and her cohorts had planned. But she'd underestimated him and, as per her usual, grossly overestimated her own intelligence. She had no notion that her own son had betrayed her. That Willis, despite her best efforts to make him nothing more than her pawn, had a far keener sense of self-preservation than maternal devotion.

His biggest concern at that moment was what had become of Peter. Willis' location was known to him, but Peter's was of far greater concern. Had the younger boy found his way to wherever Meredith and Minerva were being held?

In his dark corner, with a hat pulled low over his face to conceal his identity, he watched as she made her way into the room. She took a seat at the table that backed to the one he occupied and was neighbored by the Bow Street Runners. They would be able to hear anything that was said.

Only moments later, a familiar-looking man entered. He was dressed as he had been that day on the street and in the park. Large-framed, raw-boned and rough-looking—the man's gaze immediately flew to Charlotte and he moved unerringly toward the table she now occupied. "I'm not your errand boy to be summoned," he said, just loudly enough to make Charlotte look about with embarrassment.

"That is precisely what you are, Mr. Pfife," she answered sharply. "Now sit. We have much to discuss. Where are they now?"

"They got away. I was going after them when I saw you sashaying in 'ere," he snapped. "If you want the job done, you best let me do it!"

"Your job was to use them to lure Barrett to a place where we can finally dispose of him," Charlotte snapped. "Even now, they are rushing home to him! It's another opportunity wasted, Mr. Pfife, and we shall not get any further chances. They will close ranks and hire countless guards! What shall we do then?"

"You can 'ang for it," he said. "I'm done with this blasted country. I've got a mind to 'ead for the Americas and leave it all behind. Too many years in one place have left too many people looking to take a swipe out of me and I don't like it."

"You will not abandon me now!" Charlotte said, grabbing at the man's arm. It was a mistake on her part, an affront he would not ignore.

Pfife reached out, grasped her by the throat and hauled her up from the chair. "You've ordered me about for the last time. I done what you and your betrothed asked all those years ago. I ended the duke and all but one of 'is sons. Your man might have paid but we all know it was you... you're a curse upon men. You and all your kind."

"Women, you mean? The lot of you would achieve nothing without us!" Charlotte snapped.

"No. I mean conniving bitches," he snapped. "You obliterated an entire family. One brother murdering another along with his nephews for nothing more than a 'ollow title and money. And I did what I did because it was that or starve. I've been paying for it since. But I'm done now. I'd rather swing by the noose than deal with you anymore."

"You will swing for it, Pfife," Charlotte said. "But you will do it alone. My nephew will never allow such scandal to touch the family again. So do not test me. I can confess and plead for his mercy, but no such luxury will be afforded to you!"

At the neighboring table, the first Bow Street Runner stood up, shaking off the shapeless cloak he was wearing and brandishing a pistol. His partner followed suit. "We've heard enough. Your grace?"

Tipping back his hat, Barrett turned to face Charlotte whose complexion immediately mottled with rage. "Quite enough. Where is Peter?"

"How am I supposed to know? He is a young man about town, after all… free to come and go as he pleases."

"Answer me!" Barrett thundered at her.

"Well, I suppose he might be waiting outside the Darrow School," Charlotte answered with a very pleased smile. "Waiting for your Miss Stone, on the off chance she manages to escape. He is so very taken with her, after all."

"I did. I did manage to escape."

Barrett whirled then, catching sight of Minerva as she stood near the doors of the tavern. His relief was so instant and so overwhelming that it nearly took him to his knees. It was short-lived, however. Pfife, seizing the moment, made for the doorway and for Minerva. Before any of them could even respond, he had her by the throat. His large hand was wrapped about her slender neck in a way that left little doubt as to his dastardly intent.

"I'll snap her neck like a twig," he growled, squeezing none-too-gently to prove his point.

"You'll be dead before she hits the floor," Barrett warned, pulling one of the pistols from his coat pocket. If he lost her—he could not think about that. He could not even entertain the notion.

"You won't do a bloody thing! Just like when you were a child! I was the one what bashed you on the 'ead with that gun, I was the one who left you bleeding in the snow next to your father!" Pfife shouted. "If I could do it again, I'd only 'ave made sure to finish you off!"

Barrett was not a man who sought violence. In fact, he'd spent the better part of his life avoiding it altogether. Even holding weapons often left him feeling unsettled and just wrong. So many men went shooting for sport or enjoyed hunting. He never had. The very idea of taking a life was abhorrent to him. The deaths of his father and brothers had haunted him for so long, the violence of it and the senseless waste of it all had shaped him in ways few could understand. But in that moment, he was prepared to do something he'd never thought himself capable of—taking a life. If the opportunity presented itself, if only he had a clear shot to do so, he'd end the man and not even think twice about it.

As if she'd somehow read his mind, Minerva showed herself to be true to her word. She'd once told him she was capable of defending herself and that was apparently quite true. She brought one of her booted feet down hard on Pfife's instep while simultaneously slamming her elbow into his gut. It was just enough of a shock that she managed to pull away from him, falling to one side and landing in a tangle of tables and chairs.

Barrett leapt forward, taking Pfife to the ground. Despite the fact that the man outweighed him by nearly two stone, there was no match. One punch flew after another. Not even Minerva's shouts halted him. Only the intervention of the Bow Street Runners he'd hired, pulling him away from the unconscious man, brought him back to the moment and back to himself. It was as if the red haze of fury had simply taken him over and he'd beaten the man to a pulp before even having any awareness of his actions.

Glancing down at the beaten Pfife, his face a bloodied mess and Barrett's own knuckles equally mangled, he shook his head in confusion. Climbing to his feet, Barrett's breathing was ragged, his chest heaving with exertion and with fear. Fear because he knew that Pfife had spoken the truth. The man had been desperate and he'd had her in his grasp during that pivotal moment. It could all have gone very, very differently and they all knew it.

"You are unhurt?" he asked her.

"Yes... mild injuries incurred during the fracas, but nothing of note," she said, walking toward him where she took his hand and examined his shredded knuckles. "I am far less scathed than you at the moment."

"He could have killed you... would have," he said.

"But he did not," she stated firmly. "I am well. He is incapacitated... and it appears to be over, I think. This cannot really be it. The guilty parties confessed in an argument with one another?"

"It's always simpler than it looks, Miss," one of the Bow Street Runners explained. "Guilty folks love to talk when you give them room to do so."

"We must get to Meredith," Barrett said. "Do you have everything you need of me?"

One of the Bow Street Runners asked, "What you want us to do with her? She's right, you know? The talk—"

"I don't care. Let them talk. They will anyway," Barrett answered. "At least this time, they'll be speaking the truth." Without wasting another second, Barrett swept toward the door, taking Minerva's arm as he ushered her outside. Once on the street, before even attempting to hail a hack, he simply swept her into his arms, holding her close.

"We haven't time to waste," she protested.

"It isn't a waste. I need to know that you're here. That you're safe and real and this isn't a dream," he said. "So just give me a moment."

She relented, easing into the embrace, and relaxing against him just for a moment. "Will he hurt her? Will Peter hurt Meredith?"

"Possibly," he agreed, letting go of her reluctantly as the hack pulled over in front of them. Helping her inside, he followed suit quickly.

"How did you know?" she asked as they sped off. "How did you know where to find them?"

"Willis is not without a conscience entirely, it seems," he admitted. "He had no qualms about seeing me dead, but he balked at the murder of his younger sister. I suppose we should be thankful for that."

"Those children—those young men—they had no opportunity to be anything but what she chose to make them," Minerva reflected quietly. "She's turned them into monsters."

"There may hope for at least one of them, yet," Barrett said. "Regardless, I will not seek to see them punished so long as everyone else is safe. But Charlotte... I mean to see her punished to the full extent of the law and damn the scandal. It will be significant, Minerva."

"And that is all the more reason for you to marry well and try to restore the family name," she insisted.

"That is all the more reason to take the happiness I can find and savor it. There is no recovering from this sort of scandal. There is only moving forward... I will do that with no one but you," he insisted. "Make no mistake, Minerva, I will have no wife but you. No mother for my children but you. We will live together, we shall raise Meredith and John together... we will free those children, and finally I will free myself from Charlotte's poisonous influence."

"And if I refuse?"

"Why would you?" he demanded. "It is not because you do

not want me. It is not because you do not want to stay with those children. So that is my question. Is it only because you fear something so inconsequential as what others, whom we neither know nor care for, might say?"

MINERVA, WHEN FACED with that very bold and very direct question, was forced to answer it. Not for him. She was forced to answer it for herself. The ugly truth of it was that it had very little to do with sparing him censure for his choice of wife or even because she might have to face the uncomfortable gossip when others discovered her background. It was fear. She feared how much she wanted what he had offered her. To accept his offer— to promise to live with him and love him forever, and accept the same from him—that terrified her. Because she'd never wanted something so much that the thought of losing it left her utterly paralyzed with terror.

Remaining quiet, she felt like a coward, but she was simply unable to address it. Not yet. Once Meredith's safety was assured, and perhaps once she'd had a moment to beg for Effie's guidance, she might find her courage. For the moment, silence seemed to be the better option.

After what seemed an eternity, they left behind the dilapidated and ramshackle structures of Spitalfields and the other rookeries that bordered the river and the illicit dealings that were the hallmark of the area. They gave way to the grander and more elegant facades of Mayfair and the luxury shopping areas. There was no sign yet of the dingy hack that had sped off with Meredith inside it. Saying a quick prayer that they reached the Darrow School before her or at the very least at the same time she did, Minerva could not help but fear what Peter might do. Willis, despite his coldness, did have some feeling for his sister, at least. Peter, she was fairly certain, was incapable of having any real feeling for anyone. He was simply a consumer of things and people. If she served no purpose for him, he would discard her, but what he might do to her in temper beforehand was of great concern.

Finally, they turned onto the street and saw the hack easing to a stop before the Darrow School. Meredith was already emerging, hopping down gamely and starting toward the door at a run. Before she ever reached it, Peter emerged from the stairs that led down to the kitchen entrance and grabbed the girl up in his arms. She was screaming and wailing at him.

The driver of the hack, once more proving himself a kinder gentleman than so many in his profession, was shouting at the boy. Peter ignored him, hauling Meredith with him down the street. Where he meant to take her to or what his purpose was remained unknown.

Barrett banged on the roof of their hack, halting it before hopping out. He helped Minerva down, tossed a coin to the driver and then took off down the street at a run. Peter saw them immediately and hauled Meredith up against him more tightly. From his jacket, the boy withdrew a wicked-looking knife.

"Stop right there!" the boy shouted. "Stop, or I'll slit her throat where we stand."

Barrett, still several yards away, did as he ordered. For herself, Minerva moved along the outside of the street, getting closer to the two of them. Peter was apparently not fooled. It was such a terrifying repetition of the scene that had just played out in the tavern, only now it was Meredith in danger and she was the terrified bystander. Peter cut his eyes in her direction and gave a warning shake of his head, halting her in her tracks. Afraid of antagonizing him, she halted her progress and simply stood there, waiting for some chance to intervene.

"Peter, there is no winning in this situation. If you hurt her, here in front of all these witnesses, they will hang you for it," Barrett informed him calmly.

"I'll hang anyway. With all that Mother had us do to you,"

the boy snapped back. "You'll never let us live!"

"I will," Barrett promised. "I will. I do not hold you responsible for all that has come before. That was your mother's doing. She's done all that she could to poison your mind and make you pawns in her games. You have a chance here, Peter... a chance to leave that past behind and start fresh. But that may only happen if you let Meredith go."

Peter shook his head. "You lie!"

Barrett felt helpless. He could not charge Peter, not when the boy held a knife to Meredith's throat. But just when he thought all hope was lost, a door opened across the street. It was an infamous house, one known to every London gentleman. The private and exclusive sanctuary of the Hound of Whitehall. But the man who emerged from that house was not the Hound. The butler, for in his livery he could be nothing but, was north of middle-aged, but fearsomely built. Like a prizefighter with broad shoulders and a barrel chest, his hands swinging at his sides were the size of hams. The man approached the fray with a lightness of foot that was shocking given his size. He circled behind Peter, grasping the boy's wrist with one of his massive hands.

The element of surprise was just enough to allow Meredith to dash from Peter's side toward where Minerva awaited her. Barrett shot forward, tackling the boy to the ground. Peter struggled, but the difference in their size was simply too great. Once he was subdued entirely, Barrett used his cravat to bind the boy's hands.

The butler who had so handily intervened hauled the boy up from the pavement. "Shall I send for the watch, your grace?"

Barrett didn't ask how the man knew his address so readily, but he shook his head. "No, sir. Thank you for your intervention and your willingness to join the fray. But this is a family matter and will be handled privately."

"As you wish, your grace. I am only next door should you require further assistance," the man offered with one last warning look in Peter's direction.

"Let us get him inside," Minerva suggested. "All of us inside before the scandal grows even worse."

Unable to refute her logic, Barrett took Peter's bound hands and led him up the steps and into the Darrow School. The events of the day were growing more bizarre with each passing minute.

Chapter Twenty-Nine

I NSIDE THE SCHOOL, the girls were all agog over the events that had transpired outside. Peter was currently in the drawing room, being guarded by Barrett. Minerva had Meredith upstairs in her former room, treating the child's many scrapes and bruises. The simple and terrible truth of it seemed to be that Meredith was coping with the events of the day better than she was.

"You need to tend to your own injuries."

Minerva glanced over her shoulder to see Effie standing in the doorway. She still looked impossibly tired, but not to the point of collapse as she had been only a day earlier.

"I will get to them," Minerva answered. "How is Lord High-cliff?"

"Gone," Effie answered. "His fever broke entirely last night and he insisted that I leave him to rest myself. When I awoke this morning, the room was empty and he had taken his leave like a thief in the night. Or the morning, as it were."

There was something in Effie's tone, some note that reflected how deeply troubled she was, that prompted Minerva to quickly finish her task. Straightening Meredith's skirts, she offered the child a soft smile. "Go downstairs to the kitchen. Mrs. Wheaton will likely have a nice treat all ready for you."

Meredith gave her a look that was far more reflective of the solemn child she'd been when Minerva had first met her rather than the more playful child she'd become of late with her recent reunification with her brother. "You are only telling me that because there are things you want to say that you do not wish me to hear."

"And like all well-behaved children, you will go to the kitchen as you have been bidden," Minerva replied with an arched look, though it was still tinged with her affection for the child. She could not help but feel a kinship to Meredith, someone who had always felt so out of step with those around her.

Meredith sighed heavily, rolled her eyes, but rose from her perch and made her way to the corridor and beyond to whatever sweet Mrs. Wheaton would ply her with.

Alone with Effie, Minerva rose and turned to her. "Has he broken your heart entirely then?"

"Have you broken the duke's?"

Minerva looked away. "He told you that he proposed, didn't he?"

"He did," Effie replied, stepping deeper into the room. She collected bandages and salves from the assortment of provided supplies and approached Minerva purposefully. "He thinks I can sway you. Of course, we both know that of all my girls, none have ever been as stubborn as you. If you do not wish to marry him, nothing I could say would ever sway you."

"You once told me that my stubbornness was a fine quality and would serve me well in life," Minerva replied as she submitted to Effie's ministrations.

"And so it could. But obstinance for the sake of it, versus actually considering one's options and making a sound choice to put that stubbornness behind? That's the hallmark of foolishness, as we both well know. So the question is what you want, Minerva. Can you answer that?"

Him. She wanted him. But she could not say it. Of course, Effie knew her better than nearly everyone so she did not have to.

Effie sighed heavily and then continued. "The man I want more than anything else in the world runs from me, Minerva, because he feels he does not—that he cannot—be worthy of me. You run from the man who wants you more than anything in this world for the same reason. But you are good enough for him. You are good enough for anyone. Do not sell yourself short by assuming otherwise… to do so is to sell me short. To say that all I have done for you, all I have taught you to do for yourself… that it is not enough."

"You think I should accept him." She wanted Effie to make the choice. She wanted to have someone else to blame if it all fell apart, she realized.

"I think, Minerva, that you should accept yourself," Effie answered as she gently treated and bandaged one of the scrapes on Minerva's arm. "You are not your mother's fall from grace. You are not your father's descent into iniquity. You are simply you. And you deserve to love and be loved if that is what your heart desires."

"I love him," Minerva admitted. "I didn't mean to, but I do. He's so very kind. And he's been so alone for so long. I worry that it is only that loneliness and isolation that drew him to me… that if any woman had crossed his path who was kind to him, he might have felt the same." That admission surprised her. She'd never put into words precisely why she feared that his feelings for her would not—could not last. She feared, as Effie had suggested, that there was nothing remarkable enough about her to warrant his regard.

Effie clucked her tongue then gently cupped Minerva's face. "Then I have failed you because I have let you leave my home without ever knowing your worth. Trust in him, Minerva, until you can trust in yourself. Love is too precious to let it go… especially for such an ugly illusion."

BARRETT LOOKED AT the sulking Peter and made a decision.

Getting to his feet, he crossed to the boy and released the bonds that held his wrists.

"I could try to kill you again," Peter said.

"You could. But you will not. Despite what your mother attempted to do, Peter, I am not your enemy. I know what it's like to live under her thumb, to hear her voice in your head, whispering all those insidious things," Barrett admitted. "I lived there with her for six months. For six months, I listened to her whispering in my ear about the evil I had done, about the way I had murdered my own father and brothers. I knew. I *knew* that I had not. But it was so incessant and inescapable that I could not block it out entirely."

It was perhaps the first time that Peter looked at him with anything other than sullen resentment. There was an understanding in that moment between them.

"She promises you things," Barrett continued. "She promises that you can have all you want if you will only do as she asks. For me, she wished me to admit my guilt—when I could not, she sent me to Bedlam. If she could not make me admit it, then she would discredit me to such a degree that no one else would ever believe my innocence."

"She promised that I could have any woman I wanted... that when I had the wealth and power of the dukedom at my disposal, even without the title, it would not matter. Even Miss Stone if I chose her," Peter whispered.

"And Miss Stone's choice?" Barrett queried.

"According to Mother, that did not matter. Miss Stone, according to Mother, should have been more grateful for my attentions... does that make me a fool? Because I believed her?" the boy demanded angrily.

"No. It makes you her son. No man ever wants to think his mother is a liar... or a monster. But she was, Peter."

"I know all about her monstrosity," he replied. "Cold and cruel in one instant before being indulgent and loving in another... and all of it with no rhyme or reason. Every moment in her presence is an exercise in the torment of the unknown. Continuously working to be in her favor was the only way to survive."

It wasn't self-pity that prompted the boy's confession, Barrett realized. He was speaking as honestly as he could and Barrett recognized the truth of it. "I will help you. There is a school in the north. In Scotland. I went there myself after Highcliff took me from Bedlam. That school was the making of me. It freed my mind from the poison your mother planted in it and from the torment that Bedlam put me through. Let me send you there. Commit yourself to it and I swear, they will help you, too."

Peter's expression shuttered again, leaving only a cold and blank stare. "Do I have a choice?"

Barrett shook his head. "No. No, you do not."

"Then fine. If it's that, transportation or hanging... I'm not so stupid that I cannot see which option is in my best interest. What will become of Mother?"

"Whatever the courts deem," Barrett answered simply. "She is no longer my concern."

"It should concern you. As long as she lives, she will never give up hope. Not of claiming all that you have for herself through John. He'll never be safe so long as she lives. None of you will," Peter warned.

"You may return to the townhouse in Mayfair. Make your goodbyes to your brother. Someone will arrive for you tomorrow to take you to the school I spoke of. If you are not there... I will find you."

Peter shrugged. "I've nowhere else to go. It no longer matters."

Barrett said nothing as the boy rose to leave. But when Peter opened the door and Minerva stood just beyond it, he tensed, ready to intervene if needed. But beyond a scathing look and a hint of bitterness, Peter did not respond to her presence. He simply brushed past her and exited the Darrow School. Instantly, Barrett breathed a sigh of relief.

"Will he go to the school?"

"I think so," Barrett replied. "I think he's well aware that his options are very limited. But I am less concerned with Peter's options now than I am for my own. I asked you a very particular question earlier, Minerva. I'd like to have an answer."

"You didn't actually," she pointed out. "You spoke of what you wanted. You outlined all the reasons for it… but you never actually asked."

He stopped the unconscious pacing he'd been doing and stared at her. "Is that all that is standing in my way?"

"There is only one way to know the answer."

With his heart pounding in his chest and palms that were sweating, he asked. "Minerva, will you be my wife?"

"Yes," she said. "I will. I pray that you will never regret your choice in asking. But I know that I shall never regret my decision to say yes. You are the best man I have ever known, though I must confess that is a very limited number."

He couldn't stop the smile that pulled at his lips. "You will not mind that I hope to keep it that way? I long for my country life… for the isolation and peace of Griffingate. You will, I fear, grow bored with me."

She shook her head. "If you promise not to grow disenchanted with your very common wife, I will promise not to become bored with my very introverted husband."

"I do love you," he said. "Whatever else you might think, you must know that. From the moment I first laid eyes on you, you consumed a part of me that no one else had ever touched—a part no one else ever could."

"I love you, as well. For your kindness. For your mercy to people I would not have the strength to forgive. That you will, even now, try to see Peter given a chance to improve himself, to change his life—that speaks to the man you are and I… it humbles me that you have that capacity for kindness in you when I do not," she admitted.

"It isn't kindness… it's recognition. I know what she's done to

Peter. To Willis. I know because she tried to do the same to me. She is only capable of breaking things down, Minerva, never of building them up. I only want to give them the chance that Highcliff worked so hard to give me. What they do with it once that is done... well, that is for them to decide."

She closed the distance between them then, the door swishing closed behind her as she walked into the circle of his arms. It was the easiest and most natural feeling in the world to simply close his arms about her, to hold her close and to feel the hope of a kind of happiness he had never known simply filling him up.

"I don't want to wait. I want to marry you as soon as possible," she whispered. "I want to not be afraid to start our life together."

"I'll get a special license first thing in the morning. We'll be married within the next twenty-four hours," he promised.

"That sounds perfect."

Epilogue

Two months later

MURDEROUS DUKE VINDICATED.

The headline on the front page of the news sheet was printed in large letters, the black ink streaked from the damp. It was days old now, having come up from London to the wilds of Griffingate. But as she spread the paper out over the dining table in the breakfast room, there was a supreme sense of satisfaction for Minerva in seeing those words. The entire world would now know that he was innocent.

The article detailed the hanging of Mr. Pfife and the imprisonment of Mrs. Charlotte Entwhistle-Graves in the Bethlem Hospital for the remainder of her days. Found guilty for the murder of her husband and as a conspirator in the murders of the former duke and his eldest sons, she would never be free again.

There was a slight pang of concern, fear for what having such an infamous mother might one day mean for poor Meredith and John. Better the stain of their mother's reputation than the poison of her presence, Minerva thought.

The door opened and Barrett entered. His hair was damp from the rain, as were his clothes. He'd been out for his morning ride. He was more carefree than he had been before, more open and easy in the presence of others. But above all, he appeared to be completely happy.

"Good morning," he whispered, pausing to kiss her cheek. His gaze panned down to the paper and he frowned. "Drivel."

"Important drivel," she protested. "The world now knows you to be the man that I know... honorable, kind, innocent. It is very important."

"They don't matter," he said. "Only you... the woman who became my obsession, who consumed my every moment— awake or asleep—from the moment I first met you."

She couldn't halt the smile that always spread across her face when he said such things. "You see so much more in me than I see myself. I am not nearly so interesting nor so worthy to consume so much of your time and thought."

His gaze went hot and dark, sending a shiver through her. "That was certainly not true last night... nor was it true again this morning. You, my beautiful wife, are a seductress of unparalleled power."

Minerva's lips curved in a satisfied smirk. "I have had most excellent tutelage."

"Put your filthy gossip rag away and come upstairs with me," he urged her.

"Alas, I cannot. I have Meredith's music lessons in only a moment... and you have promised to begin teaching John how to ride. However, in an hour or so, when we are both so very tired from our labors, I see no reason that we should not indulge in a small rest to see us through the remainder of the day." She rose to her feet so that she could step fully into the circle of his arms. Leaning into the firm wall of his chest, feeling the familiar comfort and warmth of his embrace, she was overwhelmed with gratitude for what she had—for what Effie had urged her to be brave enough to reach for. Whatever came in their lives, they would have each other, and that would make it all worthwhile. "I do love you so."

He leaned in, kissing her lips instead of her cheek. As with every kiss between them, it flared hot and bright, stoking the desire that seemed ever-present in her for him.

A chorus of "ewws" sounded from the doorway, prompting them to break apart with a laugh. John and Meredith stood there, sharing matching looks of disgust.

"Must you always be doing *that*?" Meredith demanded.

"One day, Meredith," Minerva said as she stepped reluctantly away from her husband, "you will have a husband of your own and you will understand. Until then, let us go and conquer the pianoforte while your brother learns the proper way to sit a horse!"

John was off then, racing toward Barrett, babbling with excitement. Sometimes he still struggled. He struggled to find his words. He struggled at times to put them together appropriately. But most of the time, one would never know the child had been silent for years, trapped by fear of the wicked woman who would never be able to hurt him again. And all for greed. She'd hidden the boy's birth because she feared that Barrett would marry and have a child to spite her rather than letting her son inherit. Biding her time until her eldest sons were old enough to seize control of the estate at Barrett's death, she'd kept John locked away for future use, nothing more than a commodity to her. And yet that monstrous woman had produced two beautiful, resilient children who loved to the fullest extent their hearts would permit.

Impulsively, Minerva reached out and pulled Meredith into her arms, hugging the little girl tightly.

Meredith, insightful as ever, looked back at her. "There is no more danger, Minerva. We are as safe now as we ever will be."

"You're a shockingly smart girl," Minerva pointed out. "And I am so very, very lucky to have you in my life."

"And when you have another baby, will you still feel lucky to have John and me about?"

Minerva did not press her hand to her belly. It was only a thought at that point, a hope that had not yet been confirmed. Still, she strongly suspected that she was with child already. "I shall never not feel lucky to have you both, no matter how many children we are blessed with. You will be the very best big cousin ever. You will teach your little cousins all they need to know in life!"

Meredith smiled then. "I will be excellent at that. I am very good at knowing things."

For the next hour, the house rang with the sounds of music and laughter. Then it grew quiet. Quiet but peaceful and more full of love than it ever had been.

About the Author

Chasity Bowlin lives in central Kentucky with her husband and their menagerie of animals. She loves writing, loves traveling and enjoys incorporating tidbits of her actual vacations into her books. She is an avid Anglophile, loving all things British, but specifically all things Regency.

Growing up in Tennessee, spending as much time as possible with her doting grandparents, soap operas were a part of her daily existence, followed by back to back episodes of Scooby Doo. Her path to becoming a romance novelist was set when, rather than simply have her Barbie dolls cruise around in a pink convertible, they time traveled, hosted lavish dinner parties and one even had an evil twin locked in the attic.

Website: www.chasitybowlin.com

Milton Keynes UK
Ingram Content Group UK Ltd.
UKHW052324230124
436540UK00025B/991